THE
GOOD
SON

Greg Fleet is an actor, comedian, broadcaster and author. Born in Michigan, USA, his family moved to Victoria when he was aged four. He studied at Geelong Grammar School for twelve years and then attended NIDA for a year before being expelled. His acting career began opposite Nicole Kidman in 1984 and he went on to star in *Prisoner* (as 'Delivery Man No 2'), *Underbelly: Squizzy* (as Richard Buckley – Australia's most violent prisoner), and *Neighbours* (his character killed the much-loved character Daphne), as well as treading the boards as Feste in Shakespeare's *Twelfth Night* for the Melbourne Theatre Company, and developing a stand-up career that saw him acclaimed all over the world. Both here and in the UK, his comedy across TV, film, radio and theatre, and the honesty with which he speaks about his long-term drug addiction, have made him one of the most respected, beloved and in-debt stand-up comics around. Greg Fleet's hilarious and harrowing memoir, *These Things Happen*, was published in 2015.

This book is dedicated to Sunday Fleet, Roz Hammond and Ian Darling, for showing me how beautiful the world can be.

James Rogers never cried at his mother's death. But he did feel guilty for not being there when she passed. Everyone else was there, in the old people's home, by her bed. His sister, his brother, his nieces and nephews, all his mum's friends. But James wasn't there. He was with Cash Driveway, too stoned to even contemplate death, let alone actively surround himself with it.

James was thirty-five years old, tall, thin and usually didn't smoke a lot of marijuana, but he did that day, and he got way too stoned. Anyone who says, 'Well, I don't care how stoned I was, if my mother was on her death bed, I would be there' has clearly never stood around in a kitchen smoking 'Mullumbimby Madness' with Cash Driveway. Cash Driveway is a lovely man of about fifty with grey hair that is balding in the middle but active on the sides so that sometimes he looks like Einstein or a koala. And he has an uncanny ability to make people embark on noble but foolish quests. If Cash was a literary creation, he would be the Man of La Mancha, but way more out of it, bravely yet awkwardly tilting at windmills. Cash's suggestion on that day was that the two of them try to smoke themselves straight. He had a theory that if you smoked enough joints you could go full circle, from straight to extremely stoned and then somehow back to being clear-headed and capable. There were certainly flaws in the plan.

Cash Driveway is not manipulative or evil; he is a good man who just has too many questions and his search for answers is extremely infectious. Cash Driveway is an enigma. No one knows where he is from or exactly how old he is; there is very little information available about him. In fact, one of the only things that is known for sure about Cash Driveway is that his name isn't Cash Driveway.

But this story isn't about smoking dope or Cash Driveway.

It's about when to hold on and when to let go. It's about falling in love. It's about impulsive journeys to Byron Bay. But mostly, it's about James Rogers, the beautiful Sophie Glass and an amazing 76-year-old woman called Tamara Higginson.

And I very much hope you enjoy it.

The morning of Cash Driveway's failed experiment, James Rogers had been doing what he usually did. He had got up early and gone to his job cleaning a cinema in St Kilda. Like most cinemas these days it was criminally underused, which made it very easy to clean, which made this a good job. It usually took James about two hours, it paid well, and it also came with free entry to any movie, any time. While James had never aspired to being a cleaner, his deep love of cinema and his hatred of being broke made this one of the best jobs he had ever had. Sadly the cinema, the majestically named 'Majestic', was haunted by the constant threat of being shut down. It seemed that people would rather watch a film on their iPhone than go through the agony of sitting down in a comfortable chair and watching one in a building designed and built for that very purpose.

By ten that morning James was done with work and was riding his bike through the lovely streets of St Kilda, enjoying the views of the water and the early summer sun. Most of the people James knew lived in the area: a mix of artists, bartenders, writers, 'people of the night' and part-time university professors. The kind of folk who find having a glass of wine and then going out for breakfast very doable. The kind of people who don't have any need for shoe polish, ironing boards or rowing machines.

Once a week or so, James would drop in on his old fine-art tutor Cash Driveway. As James had no commitments for the rest of the day, he texted Cash and five minutes later was chaining his bike up in Cash Driveway's driveway. Cash was pretty much the only person James ever smoked dope with, but this had more to do with Cash's magnetic personality and his interest in social experiments than it did with any real desire on James' part to get wasted. If Cash Driveway had influence over James' actions, he was blissfully unaware of it and, as we have already decided that Cash is a good man and that any negative judgement from us would only muddy what are already slightly cloudy waters, I think we can safely move on.

About ten minutes into Operation Get Too Stoned, James Rogers received a text message. Or rather, he didn't. His phone received a text message from his sister, Claudia, telling him to get to the Peggy Day Aged Care Home immediately as their mother was close to death and this would be his last chance to see her. Fortunately James didn't see the message for some time. I say 'fortunately' because by now James was already extremely stoned, and dealing with the death of a loved one when you've been hanging out in Cash Driveway's kitchen could send one down quite a rabbit hole.

Considering that I told you this story wasn't about smoking dope or Cash Driveway, you may be beginning to lose faith in me as an honest narrator. Please don't. Cash Driveway and pot smoking are merely the literary equivalent of appetisers before we commence the all-you-can-eat banquet of this story.

Eventually James saw the text message from his sister and, with a sympathetic hug and three squares of rum-and-raisin chocolate from Cash Driveway, he jumped in a cab and raced to the Peggy Day Aged Care Home. He was, of course, too late, but the eternal optimist in him was saying, 'It's okay, she won't have died yet.' Meanwhile, the still slightly stoned and paranoid part of him was asking, 'Is it perverse and selfish to hope that your mother doesn't die until you are there to see it?' It was one of those situations that sounds more gruesome than it is.

By the time James ran breathlessly up the ornate stairs and into the reception area of the home, his mother had been dead for exactly ninety-three minutes. He hoped that the number ninety-three was a number his mother liked but, as we all know, if you are looking for the upside in being ninety-three minutes late to anything, you are pretty much grasping at straws.

Claudia met him in the foyer. No one had to apologise – thankfully they were not that kind of family – they just hugged and thought about their mother and what she had been and was no more. Twenty-six years ago their father had died and now their mother was gone: they had no more parents to lose.

Claudia introduced James to a young woman who had been their mother's carer in her last weeks. Her name was Sophie and she had a combination of dark hair and green eyes that James found almost impossible to look at. Her particular kind of beauty made him remember being in his early twenties. Beautiful people and beautiful heartbreak. Uncontrollable crying fits in cars out the front of beautiful houses that belonged to beautiful girls, both of which he had no doubt entered for the last time. And because Cash Driveway's (again!) experiment had only partially worn off, James found himself questioning everything. Was it wrong to be attracted to someone while your mother lay dead nearby?

As Claudia had to go pick up her children from school, she gave her little brother a kiss on the forehead. She had done this ever since he was a baby and their parents had brought him home from the hospital. Claudia was three years older than James when they were growing up and, as far as James could tell, she was always going to be three years older than him. He liked having a big sister. The kisses on the forehead made him feel safe, and in that place, at that time, he wanted all the safe feelings that he could get.

After his sister had left, Sophie asked James if he wanted to see his mother. Suddenly it all seemed very real.

'I don't know. I mean, I appreciate the offer but I think I've left it a bit late, don't you?'

'No,' said Sophie. 'People find it helps.'

'It helps? But she's dead. I'm not a doctor but I can't see anything I say or do really helping at this point.'

'Not her. You. It may help you.'

And with that Sophie took James to see his mum.

Sophie led James down a hallway and into his mother's room. There was a screen around the bed which gave James visions of racehorses, steeplechase and bad falls. Sophie asked James if he wanted her to stay and he said yes. She then pulled the screen open, stepped back and let James see his mother. She looked normal – not dead or alive, just old. Old and tired.

James sat down by his mother's bed and took her hand. He then looked to Sophie. Sophie's expression said, 'What are you looking at me for? She's your mother.' (Quite a difficult thing to convey without using words.)

James began to speak, cautiously at first but then with a building confidence. He told his mother many things that he should have told her when she was alive and quite a few things he should never have told her, not even after she was dead. Nine

of the things that he told his recently deceased mother were as
follows:

1. You were right. When I was ten I did steal that $2 coin from
   under the front doormat. I spent it on lollies.
2. Going against your advice, I once tried to eat something
   that was bigger than my own head. I failed.
3. Munty the cat did not run away. I accidentally ran him over
   in the driveway.
4. I once found a vibrator in your bedside drawer. I was
   pleased and proud of you.
5. Robbo the gardener was not gay. Claudia and I paid
   him $100 per month to tell you that he was and we all
   maintained that illusion for twelve years. Hearing you tell
   your tennis ladies, 'Well, Robbo, my gay gardener, says . . .'
   was well worth the money.
6. When I was fourteen, Dad gave me this piece of advice:
   'Never make love to a lady if there is a shovel in the room.'
   He refused to elaborate and to this day I spend large
   chunks of time wondering what he meant.
7. I hated the way you would say 'six a.m. in the morning'.
   It's either six a.m., or six in the morning. Saying six a.m.
   in the morning is ridiculous.
8. The day I had my appendix out was just laziness running
   amok. I had a history exam and I wanted to get out of
   school so I said I had a terrible tummy ache. The next thing
   I knew the doctor had me whizzed off to hospital and my
   perfectly healthy appendix was cut out. I still had to do the
   exam a few days later. It was really easy and I got a B+.

9. I loved and appreciated you far more than I ever
   let on.

Once he'd finished speaking, James sat by his mother's bed for a minute and then started to feel a little extraneous. He had just wanted to say some things, and those things had been said. He got up, none of his guilt resolved, and turned to Sophie.

'How was that?'

'Well, I guess it was fine.'

'Do you think she would have liked it? I mean, obviously the timing could have been better – but was it okay?'

Sophie led him from the room and said, 'James, only you can know that. I liked the bit about pretending the gardener was gay, though. I think she would have loved that.'

'Probably not. My mother didn't really get jokes. My sister said that Mum had her sense of humour shot off in the war.'

'War? What war was she in?'

'No. That was a joke too. I think you and my mum must have got on famously.'

Sophie took the somewhat stunned James to the staff room and made him a cup of chamomile tea. He wanted normal tea (a term that Sophie took exception to) but they were out of normal so he got chamomile. She figured it would soothe him and open his mind to a less beveragist way of thinking.

As they drank their not-normal tea, James began to express remorse for not having been there when his mother had died. People who miss the death of a loved one often assume that everyone but them has done the right thing. That by not being there at the end, they are in a very small and selfish club populated by sociopaths and those on their way to hell. Sophie knew quite the opposite to be true: that most old people died alone. A lot of families came late or did not come at all. She also knew that telling James that would probably not cheer him up.

'This sucks,' sighed a defeated James.

'Well, at the risk of sounding harsh, you are not the first person to have had this experience. You are not the first human to feel guilt.'

'It's not guilt . . . I don't feel guilty.'

'Okay then, shame. You are not the first person to feel shame.'

'Your choice of words is getting worse. I feel neither of those things,' said a clearly guilt-ridden and shame-filled James.

Sophie had seen it hundreds of times. Almost everyone who walked into the place a little late experienced what James was currently experiencing. The thing was, though, they all only went through it once. She, on the other hand, got to have her own little groundhog grief day with every one of them. Every time. She didn't drink chamomile tea for the taste.

Explaining all of this to James, Sophie surprised herself: until that very moment she had never realised the toll that watching the same kind of suffering, over and over, was taking on her, and she was a little shocked that she was opening up about this to someone she had just met. Although she didn't know it yet, one thing that both Sophie and James shared was their inability to sit on feelings or information. Some people pondered, thought about things for a long time, before giving them voice. Sophie and James were not those kinds of people. If they thought of something, they said it almost immediately. It was as though their thought patterns and speech were synced. That was the reason that they were both good at pub trivia. They made snap decisions and went with their guts. It was also the reason they were both single.

'What do the others, the "hundreds of others", what do they do about this feeling? Surely someone has worked out what to do,' said James.

'They do – nothing. They just get on with life.'

'That's not enough. I hate feeling this. You must hate going through it over and over. I want to do something to make it . . . Make it better. Is there some way out of this? You must have some answers? Or do you just make sad people weird cups of tea?'

Sophie got up and moved to the exit, as though she was about to leave. James was slightly taken aback that his calling chamomile tea 'weird' was enough to make her storm out of the room mid conversation. At her final step, though, she stopped and closed the door to the staff room, so that no one could see or hear them. She then returned to the table and her seat opposite James. She stared at him for a few seconds, trying to decide if he was worthy. In the end she looked deep into him and said:

'Well, there is one thing we could try.'

Sophie told James about a plan that she had been formulating for some time. A plan that, until he had arrived, only seemed possible in theory. In a rush of words she let him know what she had in mind.

And like a puppy in a flowerpot, it was a cute plan.

She told him that the one thing that connected the patients at the home more than anything else was an obsession with their children and a desire that they would come and visit more often — or, in a saddening number of cases, a wish that their children would visit at all.

Sophie suggested that James could visit a select number of patients. With Sophie's help, he could learn as much about their families as possible, then pretend to be the patients' sons. For a short while he'd act the role of loving long-lost child, and bring some joy to a life that would soon end.

At first the plan had hardly seemed real. But the more that the two of them talked about it, the more they realised that the idea had potential, that it had legs, that it could be done. Though probably (read definitely) illegal, it wasn't the kind of illegal where either one of them stood to benefit from it financially. It was just a great way to make a few old people very happy at the end of their lives. And, they both thought but didn't say, it was also a lovely way for James to 'say goodbye' to his real mother.

'Okay, so what do we do if some old person who thinks I'm their son suddenly gets a flash of clarity and wants to know who the fuck I am?'

'We just tell them you're a new worker here and that you have been reading to them. It's simple,' replied Sophie.

James was not completely convinced by this. 'Have you ever noticed that whenever someone describes something as simple, it usually isn't? Like assembling an IKEA bed, or trying to follow . . . a . . . complex thing?' For some reason James always went for two examples of a thing, when he usually only had one good one in his head. Consequently, his descriptive sentences often started brilliantly but then faded quite badly at the end.

'Listen, James,' said Sophie, 'I see these people going through the same things, the same emptiness every day. I honestly believe that we can do something about it, to make it better. But if you don't want to or can't go through with this, I fully understand.'

'No. I want to do it. I just want to be sure, as sure as we can be, that it will work.'

Sophie leaned across the table and smiled reassuringly at James. And a small part of him, the part that usually stopped him from falling in love, even just a little bit, with medical professionals, quivered.

The next morning, after James had finished cleaning the cinema and was locking the place up, he stopped to read a large sign in the window that had caught his eye when he first went in. It was offering the Majestic for sale to the highest bidder. To James, reading this was like reading a text message sent from your partner in which they break off your relationship. James was single and he spent more time with the Majestic than he did with anyone or anything else. This proves that the use of the girlfriend–cinema metaphor is more than simple laziness on the part of your narrator.

With a heavy heart James cycled his way to the Peggy Day Home to meet Sophie as planned. It had not been an ideal start to the day, but, although he didn't know it as he chained up his bike, things were about to improve. On greeting Sophie in her office,

he was met with the news that his application to be the facil-
ity's new care assistant had been approved. This was an exciting
development, especially as he had never applied for any such job.
James started to feel like he was in a spy movie. Most men have at
some point had that feeling, or at least wanted to have it. A selfless spy working for the greater good. James loved it, possibly a
little too much.

'So that's my cover story,' he said to Sophie. 'This is the eye of
the needle, and I'm going in deep. Tell the chaps at MI6 that I'm all
over this like treacle on porridge.'

'Maybe stop talking now, James,' Sophie said gently.

'Fair call.' James was a man who, if nothing else, was fairly good
at admitting when he was being annoying.

James filled out some forms, had his photo taken and was issued
with a laminated identity card. For the rest of that day, and for
the few days following, every time he saw Sophie he flashed his ID
at her as though he was a cop. He would then say something like
'James Rogers, Care Assistant', 'James Rogers, CA. Gumshoe for
hire' or 'James Rogers, Care Assistant. Can I have another chamomile tea? I'm developing a taste for it'. Unlike the patients at the
home, it just never got old.

Over the next couple of weeks, James spent a few hours every day
at the Peggy Day Home, and, for want of anything else to do, he
actually started behaving like a care assistant: helping out around
the place, sometimes cleaning, sometimes doing laundry or assist-
ing with meals. It was a way of getting to know the place and learn
how things operated, while, for the most part, not being seen by

the patients. Sophie began pointing out various people to James and giving him a brief run-down on who they were and why they either were or were not suitable candidates for Operation Meet Your Son.

Obviously some of the people at the home were not suitable because, while they may have been lonely and would have loved a visit from family, they remembered their children all too well. Their pain was amplified by clarity; their heartbreak was not going anywhere soon. There were also people who didn't remember their children because they didn't remember anything at all. People like Mrs Sylvia Jameson, an elegant woman of ninety. Each morning Sophie and the other staff would reintroduce themselves to her and each morning she would meet them, again, for the very first time. For James to visit Mrs Jameson as her son, someone would first have to explain to her that she had a son. That she had been married. That she had once had a life before the single day that was now her eternity. Instead James would sometimes go to Mrs Jameson as himself, and they would sit in her room and he would read to her from books and magazines. She very much enjoyed the sound of his voice, and that was enough.

A possible option, though, was Mr Angus Hill, a 92-year-old retired policeman. He had two living sons who he had not seen for many years. Unfortunately for Sophie and James, both of his sons were now in their late fifties, but – in an unforeseen turn of events that excited Sophie – it turned out that he also had three grandsons who ranged in age from twenty-seven to thirty-six.

'Maybe we should start with someone who isn't a retired cop,' said James as they watched the old man from the office window.

Then there was Madeline Ames, an 89-year-old woman who had at one time been perhaps the most respected agricultural scientist in the world. Thirty years earlier she had been a joint winner of a Nobel prize for her discovery of a mutative gene that affected domesticated but not wild pigs. Now, though, she was almost completely blind and suffering from a particularly voracious kind of Alzheimer's. Sophie told James that she often mentioned that her son Gary was coming to visit her. Gary would have been quite a few years older than James but, taking into account Professor Ames' almost total blindness and her advanced memory loss, James thought that he could pull this off.

'She's the one. It's almost too perfect,' said James.

'It is,' said Sophie. 'It won't work. You can't be Professor Ames' son.'

'What? Why not?'

'Because she doesn't have a son. She never had any children. As she is getting older and falling away from the light, she seems to have just made Gary up. Perhaps to fill a hole, I don't know.'

'So what?' said James. 'I don't care if he's real or not. I can do this. The main thing is *she* believes he's real, and if she believes he's real, he is real.'

'No. That's not how this works, if it works at all,' said Sophie. 'You pretending to be real people is going to be hard enough. But you pretending to be pretend people? That could just open up Pandora's box, and we don't want that.'

'I guess not . . . What exactly is Pandora's box?' asked James.

'I'm not exactly sure,' said Sophie. 'But it's not good. Especially when opened.'

Perhaps the most fascinating person at the Peggy Day Aged

Care Home was Mrs Jean Murphy, a kind and intelligent woman in her seventies. Each morning, she stood alone next to a huge oak tree down by the fence that separated the home from the main road. She would wait there patiently for a couple of hours, then return solemnly to her room. James found her consistent routine mildly amusing until Sophie told him her story.

At the age of thirty Mrs Murphy had given birth to twins, a boy and a girl, before suffering what we now call postnatal depression. Her husband had her committed to an asylum (perfectly acceptable spousal abuse back then). The asylum had stood on the grounds of what was now the Peggy Day Home and Mrs Murphy had moved straight from one to the other. She had never caused the doctors any problems at all but by that time she was an ageing woman with no family ties who had grown reliant on the care of others for her daily life.

'Jesus,' said James. 'Poor Mrs Murphy.'

'Oh, you have no idea.'

Sophie went on to tell James that after Mr Murphy had dumped his wife at a lunatic asylum for the heinous crime of finding it difficult to deal with twin babies, Mrs Murphy had given him a note for her children and asked that he pass it on to them when they turned eighteen. In it she told the twins that she loved them very much, and that she was sorry for not being stronger, and that all she lived for was the hope of one day seeing them again and hopefully having them back in her life. She told them that she would wait by the big oak tree in the grounds of the hospital – now the home – every day between the hours of ten and twelve, from the day of their eighteenth birthday until the day that they came to see her.

One thing that Sophie didn't know, and therefore didn't tell James, was that Mrs Murphy's husband had never given the letter to the twins. He hadn't seen the point. He remarried. He got on with his life.

These things happen.

We will return to this story.

Outside of his time at the Peggy Day Aged Care Home, James' life went on much as it had before. He still rode his bike around and saw his friends; he still had his much-loved job at the cinema, the one that actually paid him an income, although cleaning the cinema at times now felt like a detour from his primary mission.

The only person James told about his and Sophie's plan was Cash Driveway, and Cash loved the idea. He saw it as a kind of performance art, with James as Isadora Duncan (sans sports car, long scarf and getting strangled) and Sophie as some benevolent svengali. Cash also noticed that James was talking about Sophie more and more, and that pleased him. Perhaps this would end up being more than just a working relationship. Perhaps not. Guess we'll find out.

*

One Tuesday afternoon as he prepared to leave the home, Sophie ushered James into her office and, smiling, handed him a thin blue cardboard file.

'What's this?' he asked.

'Congratulations, Mr Rogers. Your training is over. What you are holding is your first assignment. Tomorrow morning Margaret Harrison's "son" Steve is going to pay her a visit.'

'Holy shit . . .'

'I know! It's pretty exciting, isn't it?'

'Holy shit. Holy fucking . . . fuck!' blurted James, displaying his advanced linguistic skills.

'This is where we see if we have lost our minds, or if we are, in fact, visionaries. Take the file home and learn all you can about Mrs Harrison, Steve and the rest of the family. How do you feel?'

'I feel great. I feel like James Bond. Should I destroy this after I've memorised its contents?'

'No. You should bring it back in the morning. It's Mrs Harrison's file.'

As the two of them got up and reached the door, James paused.

'This *is* the right thing to do, isn't it?'

'Yes,' said Sophie. 'I think so . . . I don't really know. It feels right to me.'

'Yeah, it does. It feels right,' replied James with an easy smile.

And so they decided to carry on with the plan, knowing that in the past more important people than them had based much more crucial decisions on far flimsier premises.

*

That night James stopped at the Thai place on the corner of his block and bought a takeaway beef rendang. The place was called Thai-tanic and was owned and run by a man called Graham. When he got home, he took the rendang and the blue file on Mrs Harrison to his favourite place in his apartment: his king-sized, memory-foam-clad bed. It had been a gift from his art-school friends when he announced that he and his Spanish girlfriend, Renée, were getting married. When three weeks later Renée announced that she was leaving him for a visiting American installation artist and moving to New York City, his friends worried that the huge bed would serve as a constant reminder of how all alone he now was. It didn't. Instead, James told them, it served as a constant reminder that he now had a really excellent bed. James Rogers was certainly a glass-half-full kind of guy.

As he lay on the bed holding Mrs Harrison's file he thought again about the ethics of what he and Sophie were embarking on. The fact that he now worked at the home certainly lessened the illegality of the venture, and the fact that the two of them genuinely wanted to make the old people happy seemed to legitimise their actions beyond any kind of moral examination. His main concern was causing trouble for Sophie, having their actions make her lose her job. A job she clearly loved. But in the end he decided that they would be okay. They were doing this because they cared and sometime, somewhere, someone had written something about the pure of heart and how good things came to them. Well in this case James and Sophie were the pure of heart, and that meant that everything was going to be all right. He opened the file and started reading.

The first few pages were medical records, from which James gleaned that Margaret June Harrison was eighty and, aside from

Alzheimer's disease, she was suffering from the various ailments that can afflict a woman of her years, including badly failing sight and hearing.

What followed was, to James Rogers, pure gold: Mrs Harrison's life history forms, or her 'LAGS' as the staff mysteriously called them. LAGS were standard information that the Peggy Day Home kept on every patient. The families usually filled them out and they could vary in length from a few sentences to thirty-three pages (the length of the longest, describing Franz Camera, ninety-one, whose son was, not surprisingly, an unpublished writer). Mrs Harrison's LAGS were twelve pages long, and to James each of those pages was another part of her. Like twelve photographs taken at various crucial moments in her life. Whoever wrote this, thought James, took a lot of time in its construction. They obviously cared deeply for Mrs Harrison. So where were they now?

Margaret Harrison and her husband, Sam (deceased), had raised three children, Kate, Tegan and Steven. By all accounts they were a loving, happy unit. But the only one of the Harrison children that the home had any contact with was Kate, fifty-six, who now lived in Singapore with her own family. Kate was a good daughter who paid her mother's bills on time and sent monthly emails to check on her condition, but she had only made the trip back to Melbourne twice in the past decade.

Steven (who James was going to become the next day) was something of a mystery. He was forty-two years old and had worked in various countries as an engineer in the energy sector, mostly on offshore oil rigs. The Peggy Day Aged Care Home had never had any dealings with Steven and Sophie had no idea what he looked like. He was, as far as they could tell, just a name and a job.

There was a photo of Kate, though. James looked at it for a few minutes and decided that he could convincingly pass as her brother. James had the same colouring as the woman in the picture and even similar features. He was starting to feel confident. Thinking further, he decided that Steven was probably about 187 centimetres tall. There will be no prizes given to anyone who has worked out that 187 centimetres is exactly how tall James was.

Glass half full.

After reading the rest of Mrs Harrison's LAGS, James put down the blue folder and felt good about the whole plan. Next to his bed was a picture of a dog and he turned to it with a smile. It was Charlie Girl, the Jack Russell–dachshund cross who had been James' constant companion from his early twenties until the previous summer when she had died. James used to talk to Charlie Girl as though she was a person and he now treated her picture the same way.

'Charlie Girl, I reckon this is going to go like clockwork. Don't you? I mean, I can act, a bit. Gravedigger in *Hamlet* in Year Eleven? I smashed that, so I can do this. I've read Mrs Harrison's LAGS, I look quite a bit like her daughter, so unless Steven was adopted I will be absolu— Holy shit! What if he *was* adopted? What if he was adopted from a Chinese family? How am I going to explain my total lack of Chineseness? He won't have been Chinese . . . Will he, Charlie Girl?'

In the picture, Charlie Girl was standing on a beach in Torquay with a ball in her mouth, looking at the camera. She was as happy as a clam, a brown-and-white, long-haired, four-legged clam. James had loved her so much and, for twelve great years, she had loved him right back. He picked up her picture, took a deep breath and smiled.

'Yeah, Charlie Girl, you're right, Steve's probably not Chinese. I know. I'm just being paranoid – and now I'm taking life advice from a photograph. I miss you, crazy pup.'

James thought about going online and learning as much as possible about Chinese adoption laws but instead he put down the picture of his dog and drifted off into dreams of himself, Sophie and Charlie Girl all working on an oil rig somewhere in the Gulf of Mexico.

For James, the actual meeting with Mrs Harrison was, like many 'first times', far overshadowed by the anticipation. That build-up was like the ticking of a clock on an old-school bomb.

James had rarely felt more present or focused than he did on the walk from Sophie's office, down two corridors, to Mrs Harrison's room. He never wore a uniform, so the sight of him and Sophie walking the halls of the Peggy Day Home, him in street clothes, was quite normal. The fact that he was dressed slightly more 'mining engineer' than usual went unnoticed.

Outside Mrs Harrison's door, Sophie stood in front of James, looked deep into his eyes and said, rather seriously, 'You can do this.'

Then Sophie opened the door to the room and announced, 'Hello, Mrs Harrison. Your son Steven is here to see you!'

Mrs Harrison sat propped up in bed, frailty wrapped in antici-pation. 'Steven,' she said, her smile almost forcing her back to her youth. 'You look wonderful!'

'So do you, Mum!' James' voice came out more like a squeak than he had intended, and quite suddenly he realised that he was far more nervous than he had thought he would be.

He leaned down and kissed Mrs Harrison on the cheek.

'No, I don't. I look terrible,' she said, glancing over to where Sophie stood tingling with how well it was going. 'Steven was always a very kind boy, but an appalling liar. I once tried to teach him to lie, but sadly he just couldn't do it.'

'Oh, stop it, Mum. I can lie; I just don't.' James was easing into being Steven, the put-upon son. The loving but petulant child. Sophie wondered how much of this was acting and how much of it was just James being a man-child and simply not wanting to be told what to do by his mother. Any mother. But whatever he was doing it was certainly working and it took all of Sophie's self-control not to start applauding.

James stood at the side of Mrs Harrison's bed. She took his hands in hers. 'Well, sit down, Steven. I haven't seen you in months, and you're not going to spend this visit standing to attention like last time!' Sophie and James shot each other a concerned glance. Mrs Harrison hadn't seen Steven for *years*, and he'd certainly never been to the home. Not once.

Sophie nodded encouragingly and James did as he was told. Was this actually working? Sophie seemed to think it was, and if Sophie thought it was . . . He sat next to Mrs Harrison and her hand gripped his as though she never wanted him to leave.

Her hand felt happy and, after all, wasn't that the whole point of this?

'Now, tell me all about your work and the oil rigs,' she said, and then to Sophie: 'He's an engineer, don't you know?'

'Mum, it's all been very exciting. I've just flown in from a rig off the coast of Mexico. We had a huge oil fire there and they had to shut her down for a couple of weeks.'

A sudden wave of panic flew through Sophie; James was going off script. He was going to screw this up. She should have known that things were going too well.

'Oh dear,' said Mrs Harrison. 'What's its name?'

'What's what's name, Mum?'

'The rig. What is the rig called?'

'Oh, the rig . . . She's called the Machu . . . Picchu . . . Express . . . Yes. The Machu Picchu Express. She is an absolute beauty – when she's not on fire.'

'How exciting! The Machu Picchu Express. It sounds like a train!'

'Yes, it certainly does. A train . . . But tell me about you, Mum. How are they treating you here? That Sophie seems a little severe.'

'No, they're treating me very well. Sophie is wonderful!'

Sophie smiled from the corner, relieved that things were getting back on track.

'I don't know, Mum, she reminds me a bit of Nurse Ratched from *One Flew Over the Cuckoo's Nest*,' said James, sneaking a look at Sophie and clearly enjoying himself.

'Oh be quiet, Steven. I think you have a crush on her,' Mrs Harrison replied.

'No I don't!' said James, suddenly looking and sounding about twelve years old.

'I think he does,' said Mrs Harrison sagely to Sophie. 'He is always mean to the girls he likes.'

'Mum!' This was getting too real all of a sudden for James.

The visit flew by in an exchange of affectionate banter, and the excitement in the room was shared by all three of the people present. Eventually James leaned down and kissed Mrs Harrison on the cheek again.

'I better go, Mum, but I'll be back to see you next week.'

'Oh, Steven, I'm so very proud of you. I could not have hoped for a better son.'

When the two of them got back to the office and Sophie shut the door, there was a single second's silence before they erupted into a mini party. Jumping around, whooping, high-fiving, even a couple of slightly awkward hugs.

'How was it?' asked James. 'Was it okay?'

'It was sublime,' replied Sophie, who was looking into James' eyes as though she could see something that up until then had been shrouded in a fog. A look that spoke of trust. 'You were amazing.'

'It was great. It was way easier than I thought it would be. I did kind of panic at the start . . .'

'I saw that,' said Sophie. 'But then you just punched on through. You were surprisingly impressive.'

'Yes,' said James theatrically, 'I was rather impressive, wasn't I?'

'Except for the Machu Picchu Express bit. What was that?'

James took out his phone and starting looking for something, petulantly, clearly not enjoying being chastised. 'I was improvising!

The Machu Picchu Express was the first thing that came to mind. It was *fine*.'

'It was dangerous, is what it was. What if she somehow finds out that it doesn't exist? I mean, I'm sure we can handle it, but don't do that again. We have to generalise. Crazy specifics like that could screw the whole thing up.'

'Okay,' he said. 'I get it, stick to the plan.' Downtrodden, he turned to leave, and then stopped, a smile that threatened to engulf the room spreading across his face.

'There is one thing I thought you might like to see . . .' He handed Sophie his phone, which was open to an online news site, with a headline that read:

OIL RIG FIRE SHUTS DOWN PRODUCTION IN GULF, MACHU PICCHU EXPRESS EXTENSIVELY DAMAGED

The story went on to tell about how the Machu Picchu Express, a modern, top-of-the-line rig, had caught fire and been damaged, but fortunately without the loss of life.

Sophie read the piece and then, though trying not to, started to laugh. He'd been telling the truth. As she handed him back his phone she said, 'James, you shit. You look just a trifle self-satisfied.'

'I prefer to call it "organised",' he smirked.

'Come here,' she said, her arms open wide, genuine affection shining in her eyes. Was she about to kiss him? The three steps he took to reach her were loaded with possibilities and seemed to take years. When he stood in front of her she placed one hand on his shoulder and did something quite unexpected. She punched him, hard, on the bicep.

'Ow! That wasn't what I had in mind,' he said.

'Let's call it a day of surprises,' Sophie replied.

The punch and the Machu Picchu Express appeared to have brought them even closer together.

'I think I'm starting to like you, James Rogers,' said Sophie.

'I'm way ahead of you. And if all it takes to gain your affection is the occasional punch in the arm – please, punch away!'

As James got to the door and turned to leave they exchanged smiles. The kind of warm smiles that tell you things are going to be okay.

And who knows, maybe this time they really would be.

Dr Alexander Harvey, who was ninety-six years old and had been at the Peggy Day Home for twelve years, was next on Sophie's list. He'd been a surgeon in the Korean War and then worked at the Prince Alfred Hospital, but now he was losing his memory and balance and had extremely limited sight. Sophie admired him because, despite everything he'd been through, Dr Harvey was still one of the most energetic people in the home – and without doubt he had the best sense of humour of any of her patients.

He loved to tell jokes (although he never called them jokes – common names were, it seemed, not his thing). He especially liked jokes with a medical theme, which were usually quite complex and very funny. Because of his failing memory, though, Sophie knew that he, like many of our prime ministers, would one day start a joke and not be able to finish it.

One morning, for example, Sophie saw him completing a cross-word puzzle in the recreation room and went to his left side, his 'good' side, to talk to him.

'Morning, Dr Harvey. Do you know a two-letter word for handsome?'

'Me,' replied the old man, smiling. 'That's easy, it was in yesterday's *Times*.'

'Of course it was,' said Sophie, 'because it's the truth.'

'Would you care to experience an amusing inquiry?' (The doctor's word du jour for joke.)

'Of course I would, Doctor. I love you for your mind just as much as for your impressive physique.'

Sophie sat down in the chair next to him.

'All right, my friend. What do you call the instrument that a doctor uses to remove all signs of hope and positivity from a patient?'

'Wow, Doc, you don't mind going straight to the grim stuff, do you? Okay, all signs of hope and positivity . . . Can you give me a hint?'

A change had come over Dr Harvey. His witty expression had been replaced by one of confusion.

'I'm sorry, what?' he asked.

'A hint? Can you give me a hint?'

'My dear girl, I really have no idea what you're talking about.' Suddenly he was a picture of contained panic. 'I think I need to go back to my room now.'

Sophie's heart dropped. This was what she had feared. What she had expected.

'Of course, Doctor. I'll have someone take you straight back.'

'Why were you asking me about hints? Hints at what? What is it that you think I've done?' He was growing increasingly agitated and had that look of being lost that you only ever see on the faces of the very young or the very old.

'Nothing, it was a joke . . . It was my mistake. I'll have Malcolm take you back to your room. I'm very sorry.'

Sophie turned away to attract the attention of Malcolm, a genius musician who worked at the Peggy Day Home as an orderly to supplement the meagre income that the majority of great musicians receive. Before she had time to get Malcolm's attention, though, Dr Harvey's hand shot out and grabbed her by the wrist.

She was shocked.

She spun around just in time to see a huge smile spread across his face and to watch him stifle a surprisingly big laugh. Sophie was completely dumbfounded. The old man collected himself and began to speak.

'Oh, Sophie. I am so very sorry. I don't know what came over me. But you walked straight into that!' His delight was palpable.

Sophie was aghast. 'Doctor Harvey! You . . .' Suddenly she was laughing too. 'That was extremely inappropriate.'

'Yes, my dear, yes it was, but it was also extremely funny. I may be old and I may be losing it but I haven't lost it yet. In fact, if anyone around here is getting soft, I'd say it's you. Toughen up, old girl; the medical business can be a cruel mistress.'

His face: the cat, the cream.

To Sophie, his smile shone like the lights of a great hotel after a long and tedious car trip. These brief moments of joy were what kept her working in an environment where all too often heartbreak and tragedy were the order of the day.

As she walked away, she turned back to him and said, 'The bill . . . The instrument that a doctor uses to remove all signs of hope and positivity – it's the bill.'

Dr Harvey was suitably impressed. 'There may well be hope for you yet.'

He went back to the *Times* crossword. Sophie went back to the world. Both destinations were cryptic.

That night James Rogers went home and did his research. He skimmed Dr Harvey's file but kept returning to the part where Dr Harvey served as a medic in the Korean War. Wars, noted James, often have very positive and even cheerful names. The 'War of the Roses' or the 'Great War' (a war that history has shown us was not 'great' at all, but actually rather 'shit'). After a couple of wines James ruefully noted that there had never been a war called the 'I got shot in the side of the face and died in the mud behind a chook shed, thousands of miles from my home and my loved ones war'. But maybe, he thought, that was just implied. Maybe that is the small print for all wars, no matter how rosy or great we are told they are.

According to the LAGS, Dr Harvey's wife, Linda, had come to the Peggy Day Home with her husband twelve years ago and

then died in her sleep four years later. Their only children were
the apparently much doted on twin boys, Michael and Finn. The
Harvey clan were a tight family who prized education, travelled
the world, and leaned into life in a way that only those who are
truly loved and financially secure can. Not with a swagger, but with
an ease, or at least that's how it seemed to James as he read. But then
it all came crashing down.

When the twins were nineteen, Michael and Finn had been
travelling in a car heading down the coast for what was to be
one more in an endless string of university parties. There was
drinking, an accident, and the car rolled. Michael and two of
the other passengers were killed instantly. Finn was the only
survivor.

James dropped the file into his lap. He looked up at the
picture of Charlie Girl on the beach with the ball in her mouth.

'Jesus, Charlie Girl. Sometimes life is just . . . mean.'

There was no mention of Finn ever having visited his parents at
the Peggy Day centre. Clearly the accident had thrown acid onto
what had once been an idyllic family portrait.

Dr Harvey had often told Sophie that what he wanted more
than anything in the world was to see Finn again before his time
was up. To one last time see his family, his blood, his only surviving
son. So tomorrow James was going to be Finn. He and Sophie were
going to grant the dying surgeon his last wish and hopefully give
joy to someone who had seen so much pain.

There was absolutely nothing else in the file about Finn after
the death of his brother. No pictures, no education or work history;
nothing. James would be flying blind. And playing someone years
older than he was.

That night after James Rogers went to bed, he dreamed of Cash Driveway, Charlie Girl and Dr Harvey fighting in the trenches of World War I. In his dream a loudspeaker was playing the theme song from *M*A*S*H*, 'Suicide is Painless'. It was some dream.

The next morning James got up early as he had to meet Sophie, to run through the plan, and then to become Finn Harvey. He had noticed that since meeting Sophie he was taking longer to get ready each day. Where once he would have just rolled out of bed, thrown on any old clothes, cleaned the cinemas and maybe headed over to Cash Driveway's place, now he was spending a long time in the shower, using new and assorted body scrubs and shampoos. He was shaving more often, plucking his nose hairs and trying on various shirts before deciding which one to wear. That morning, he looked in the mirror and, after at the last minute rejecting a beret, decided that he liked what he saw. He hoped Sophie would feel the same way.

*

Sophie had got to work early that morning to check that everything was in order for that day's engagement. She and James had discussed shutdown plans for if things went to shit during one of the 'reunions'. They had decided that if one of the patients seemed to know that what was happening was bogus, if they didn't buy what James and Sophie were selling, the two of them needed a way to retreat from the plan while causing the least amount of distress. The cleanest and simplest way to do this was what they called Plan B. If someone were to sit up in bed, look at James and declare, 'Who are you? You're not my son!' Sophie would quickly glance down at her clipboard and say to James, 'Oh, I am so terribly sorry. This is my fault. Steven, your mother is in room 313 not room 212. I'm so sorry. This is Mrs Jennings, not Mrs Jackson.' James would then politely bid them farewell and be quickly ushered out into the relative safety of the hallway.

Plan B was obviously not ideal, though, because of the potential to cause upset and because of the extensive explanations that would necessarily ensue. For this reason, it was decided that James would never instigate conversation with his 'relative'. It was easier and better for all concerned if the patient was the one to make the first overture. If James were to enter the patient's room, and that patient was to smile and say, 'Tim! Oh, Tim, my boy. Come in, sit down,' that was the gold standard of introductions. If James and Sophie could pull off that kind of beginning to a 'reunion', assuming they had done their research and that James bore enough resemblance to whoever he was pretending to be, assuming they had picked the right patient, and that patient wanted to believe (because, after all, if James and Sophie were selling anything, it was belief), the two of them were sure things would run smoothly. If, however, the first thing to come out of a patient's mouth when James entered the room was 'That's not my son. My son is a six foot seven Sri Lankan man who had his left hand amputated', Plan B would swing into full effect and that meeting would be shut down fast.

Sophie went to the little kitchenette and started making herself a cup of tea. Through the window over the sink she could see Mrs Murphy making her way out to the oak tree for her daily vigil. James entered the office behind her.

'Good morning, fuck face,' came his voice.

'Hi, shit head' was Sophie's reply.

They had evolved to the point where they had abusive nicknames for each other. To James it was a very good sign. All of his relationships had begun with he and his partner giving each other insulting nicknames. There had been Rabbit Face and Monkey Girl, Stick Woman and the Weasel, Stalin and Idiot Boy, even Gulag and Ebola. Sometimes James thought that all great relationships had to have had an abusive-nickname phase. Then again, none of James' relationships had lasted longer than six months, so in many ways the jury was still out on this one.

Sophie continued to gaze at the old woman by the tree.

'Mrs Murphy?' asked James.

'Today and every day.' Sophie's voice was full of resigned sorrow.

James came and stood behind his friend.

'It must be ten a.m. She's like a clock, Mrs Murphy.'

'Yes,' said Sophie, 'a heartbreaking clock. Do you want a cup of tea? I'm having chamomile but we have got "normal" now.'

'No. I'll join you in a cup of "abnormal" tea, if you don't mind. I've got to admit I'm developing quite a taste for it.'

'I knew you would,' said Sophie with a smug grin.

He wasn't. He didn't like chamomile tea at all. He preferred coffee to tea. And he preferred normal tea to abnormal tea. To James, chamomile tea tasted like hot water poured over straw. But as Sophie handed him his cup he smiled and thanked her. It can be astounding to see the sacrifices that some people will make.

They both sat down at Sophie's desk, she on the boss side of the desk, he on the employee side.

'How did you go with Dr Harvey's LAGS?' she asked him.

'Great,' he said, handing the file back to her. 'But I'm still a little nervous about winging it as Finn. I mean, we know virtually nothing about him. No pictures. No history. All we know is that he travelled a lot when he was young and he survived the car crash in which his twin brother died. What if I am nothing like Finn? I mean, I'm so much younger than him.'

'Don't worry about it. Just stay more than a foot away from his face, and be vague. It's all about the first couple of seconds. If he likes the first bite, he'll finish the dessert.'

'He'll finish the dessert?' said James, impressed. 'Where did you hear that?'

'I didn't,' said Sophie. 'I just made it up.'

'You rock,' said James, before taking a huge swig of chamomile tea and not wincing. Maybe he was starting to like it after all.

Ten minutes later, their tea finished, Sophie looked at the clock. 'It's time. You ready?'

'I guess I am,' said James, feeling that special combination of thrilled and terrified that only trying to pull off something like this can make you feel. 'He's in his room? He knows Finn is coming?'

'He sure does. It's all he's been talking about for the last day and a half. I don't think I've ever seen him so excited.'

They left the office and started walking towards Dr Harvey's room. To James this was like the pregame ritual before a big football match. The office was like the dressing room, and walking the corridor was like moving down the tunnel and into the race. Entering the patient's room was like emerging from under the grandstand and out onto the MCG: once he was in there he just had to hope that he played smart and played committed. He had to give 110 per cent. James loved sport but he found that the numbers thrown around by football people often bore very little resemblance to actual mathematics. He recalled reading about a famous American football coach who had once said that football was '75 per cent mental and the other half physical'. In any case, James was ready to give his all for the team. A very small team of two. If he was the star player, Sophie was his super coach, and for them to win they both had to play their parts.

They reached the door to Dr Harvey's room. Sophie put her hand on James' shoulder and then gently brought it up to his cheek. 'You all good, champ?'

James turned his face away from her hand, feeling suddenly flushed. 'I'm good, coach. Just put me in the game.'

With that Sophie opened the door. It was showtime, folks.

When they entered his room, Dr Harvey was propped up in bed doing the crossword. Sophie announced, 'Dr Harvey, your son is here.'

The old man put down the newspaper, and looked up towards the ceiling or possibly the heavens, almost as though praying, or hoping for something, and said, 'He certainly is. Finn . . . Just look at you.'

'Hi, Dad. How do I look?' asked James.

'I don't know, son, I can't see you. It was rhetorical. How *do* you look? Are you wearing a hat?'

'No. I was going to wear a beret but I thought that might look stupid.'

'It certainly would have. Hats are for idiots and berets are for fools,' replied Dr Harvey. 'Finn, my boy, I am dying. I am a very old man and I have done pretty much everything in my life that I've wanted to do. But there has been one thing that I wanted more than anything else, and that was to speak to you. There are many things that I've wanted to say but we have so little time so I will just tell you the important things.'

James and Sophie exchanged glances. This was going perfectly.

'Oh, Dad, there are so many things that I've wanted to tell you as well,' said James.

'Let me finish. We have a lot to discuss, you and I, and here, today, I'd like to deal with that. To clear the decks, as it were. For my own sake, I would like a fresh start. Or a fresh finish.'

'Of course, Dad.'

A strange look came over Dr Harvey's face – a smile but kind of a cruel smile.

'A fresh start,' repeated James. 'That's what I want too.'

'Oh shut up, Finn. I don't care what you want. Did you come because you wanted to resolve our long-running mutual hatred? Or was it simply because you knew that I was dying and you wanted me to leave you my house and my money?'

'No, Dad. I don't wan—'

'*Shut* up. Don't talk. You are just going to stand there. You are going to stand there and you are going to listen.'

For a second James thought the old man might be joking, but not Sophie. She somehow knew straight away that he was being serious. Deadly serious.

The train had gone suddenly, unexpectedly off the rails and James couldn't even catch Sophie's eye. It was as if she was hypnotised, staring at Dr Harvey, compelled by what he was saying and by how chilling he had become. There was no contingency for this.

Dr Harvey clearly believed that James was in fact his son, but the old man was raining hellfire down upon him, and seemed to be enjoying it very much. James had no choice but to carry on and see where this led.

'You get nothing, you vacuous leech. My house and my money I have left to this place. The people here, including this young woman –' he looked to Sophie '– treated your mother and I with dignity and grace. But that is not why I am leaving them everything. I am leaving them everything purely so that you cannot have any of it. In this last year the only thing that has excited me about dying, aside from the inherent mystery of it all, is knowing that my death would not benefit you financially in any way. That you would get zero. Nothing. Or, as they say on *The Price is Right*, "Bah-bow".'

'That's *Family Feud*,' said James, rapidly losing patience with the old man.

'*Shut up*, Finn! You are a coward and an embarrassment, and that's all you've ever been. I never waste time wondering what kind of a son Michael would've been if you had died in the crash instead of him. He would've been a better man than you. *Far* better. Stronger. Smarter. Braver. He would have made your mother and I —'

'Fuck you!' James exploded, shocking himself with the outburst. 'I'm *glad* you're dying. I don't want your money; I never did. I just wanted a father!'

The train had not only left the tracks, it was now engulfed in flames. This time it was Sophie who couldn't catch James' eye. He was unreachable.

'Jesus fucking Christ, Dad,' he went on. 'Have you got any idea what it was like growing up with you? Have you got any idea what it was like after Michael? Mum was great, but you? You were a

24/7 horror show of self-indulgence, with your tedious Korean War stories. You know what? Fuck you, and fuck the Korean War. Fuck *M*A*S*H*. Fuck Hawkeye. Fuck everything!'

Dr Harvey began a slow handclap from his bed. 'Oh bravo, son, bravo. Now *that* is the Finn I have known and grown to despise.'

Sophie jumped in (far too late if you ask me, but she did finally jump in), opening the door and trying to push an enraged James back out into the relative safety of the corridor.

'Okay, gentlemen. I think that's enough for today. Everyone is getting a little heated . . .'

But Dr Harvey wasn't done yet.

'Get out, Finn,' spat Dr Harvey. 'You are no longer my son.'

'You know what, old man? I never was!' shouted James as he was bundled out of the room.

Sophie was now between him and Dr Harvey, pushing hard on James' chest. As she pulled the door shut behind them James managed one last 'You old *fuck*!'

Suddenly James found himself back in the corridor, back in the tunnel, heading back to the change rooms. The game was over and he was pretty sure his team had just lost.

When Sophie spoke it was with barely contained rage. 'Meet me in the office in three minutes. If you go back into Dr Harvey's room, I will fucking kill you.' With that she stormed to the end of the corridor, never looking back, and disappeared around a corner. Seconds later James heard her office door open, then slam shut and her scream the solitary word '*SHIT!*'

If James had been wearing a tie, at that moment, he definitely would have loosened it.

*

As the narrator I feel it is beholden upon me at this point to tell you that, while James and Sophie were good at what they were doing, this whole 'pretending to be other people's sons' thing was an unproven science. There was no textbook for what they were doing. And because of that, things wouldn't always go the way they expected them to. Sometimes it would be a cakewalk. Everything would fall into place as though it were the easiest thing in the world. But of course the reverse was also true. Sometimes something completely unforeseen would happen, and, as it had with Dr Harvey, very quickly the whole thing would go off the rails like a massive steam train in an old western movie. The shrieking of passengers and the rending of steel girders – never a good thing. This was the kind of screw-up that would make less committed people think about abandoning the whole project.

I know I'm only the narrator, but I think my train crash metaphor is a good one. And like an actual train crash, James and Sophie didn't know whether to look, or to look away. In any case, let's crack on, shall we?

Toot-toot, all aboard.

James opened the door to the office and stepped inside. Sophie was looking out the window and her shoulders seemed to be heaving.

'Soph, are you okay? Are you crying?' he asked, horrified.

'No, James, I'm not crying. I'm just fucking furious.' She turned around to look at him. When he saw her face he immediately wished that she was crying. Causing Sophie to cry would have been a terrible thing, but causing Sophie to be this angry? That was a whole new level of hell.

'What were you *thinking*?'

'I wish you were crying,' whispered James.

'What?' said Sophie.

'You saw what he was doing, heard the things he said – he is a fucking maniac! He only wanted to see Finn so he could say vile and fucked-up things to him. And I don't let anyone talk to me like that!'

'He wasn't talking to you, idiot. He was talking to *Finn*.'

'Well, no one talks to Finn that way. Not while I'm in the room. Finn is a good guy!'

'How do you know that, James? We know nothing about him. For all you know Finn is a serial killer or a rapist.'

'He is not a rapist! He sometimes wears a beret. Rapists don't wear berets.' But from the look on Sophie's face, now was not the time to try being funny about hats . . . 'Look, Dr Harvey was being a complete arsehole and I responded the way a son would respond in the real world.'

'But this is not the real world, James. That's not what we are building. We are walking in their worlds, their lives, not our own. It's not about us, about you – it's about them. If we make them feel great and they love us, hooray! But if they, for whatever reason, get dark and angry and hateful? We have to eat that up too. We're here to give them what they need. If they need to be angry, you tolerate their anger. If they need to hate you, you tolerate that too.'

They stood facing each other, taking each other in. James looked suitably chastised, and was ready to fall on his sword. He knew he had fucked up. His sudden explosion at the old man hadn't just taken Sophie by surprise; it had shocked him as well. James usually kept a lid on his anger but he was starting to see that maybe that lid was very poorly screwed on. Cash Driveway had often remarked that in a crisis loud, shouty people were relatively easy to handle. You knew, very clearly, where they were coming from. It was the seemingly cruisy, happy people who were the real wildcards. When shit went south, which it sometimes did, you had no way of predicting just how loco they would get.

'Sophie,' said a contrite James, 'I swear that will never happen again. Okay?'

She came towards him and took his hand, holding it in both of hers.

'Oh, James, I know. I know it won't happen again. And you know what else I know?'

'What?'

'He was a complete shit in there,' smiled Sophie.

'He certainly was,' said James. 'He was Shitty McShitface the third.' They were both smiling now.

In the next chapter, something unexpected happens. It's not earth-shattering but it is unexpected. Try to guess what it is – I bet you can't. This little bit of narration is designed to make you read on. You know, 'One more chapter before bed'. That type of thing. My publisher told me to do it and, frankly, I think it's a good idea.

The morning after the Dr Harvey fiasco, James dropped in to Cash Driveway's house. They were drinking coffee in Cash's kitchen and telling each other stories; James about Dr Harvey, Cash about the difference between the colours burnt orange and sienna. Cash told James about a study that he'd read where in an American maximum-security prison the authorities had painted all of the walls pink. The colour pink, it seemed, had a very relaxing effect on the inmates; inmates who had previously been what Cash described as 'extremely stabby'.

'Maybe I should come down to the old people's home and paint Dr Harvey's walls burnt orange,' suggested Cash.

'Maybe,' said James. 'How do you think that would affect him?'

'I have no idea. It would probably make him demand more citrus fruit. I'll give it some thought.'

It was then that James noticed the boxes. It was not unusual for Cash to have boxes, or anything for that matter, scattered around his house. But these boxes seemed to James to be filled with things that used to be on Cash's walls or on his desk or shelves.

'What's with the boxes, Cash?' asked James, prepared for virtually any answer.

'I'm packing up,' said Cash. 'I have to leave. It would seem that all adequate things must come to an end.' Cash was exuding a legitimate sense of regret, something James was not used to from him. He also looked tired, and that was definitely not something that Cash ever showed, or, as far as James knew, ever even felt.

'But why? Why do you have to leave?'

'There was an issue with the rent. Apparently I didn't pay it.' Using words like 'issue' and 'apparently' made it all sound like a big mistake; which, strangely, it was.

'What? Didn't pay it for how long?' James asked.

'As near as I can work out, about seventeen months.' Cash looked so casual as he said this, he may as well have been saying, 'Oh, six days.'

'*What?* Cash! Seventeen months? Why not?' If Cash wasn't going to panic about this, James certainly was. He looked as though he had been slapped.

'I think I just forgot. I forgot, and no one reminded me, so the whole thing just kind of snowballed. But snowballed very quietly . . . Anyway, early last week the real estate guy came over and told me that I owed them $28 900.'

'Twenty-eight . . . *What?* What happened? What did you tell him?'

'Well, for a start, the guy was really surprised that I was still here. I think they assume that if somebody racks up that kind of bill, they will have already split. And aside from the shock of me still being here, when he told me how much I owed, I think he assumed that I would either make a run for it or just fall over and start weeping.'

'Did you? I would've gone for the weeping.'

'No. Strangely, for probably the first time in my life, I have that much and more in the bank. I just told him, "Oh, I'm sorry. I've been really busy and I totally forgot to pay you. It was $28 900, yes? I can transfer that to you now or if you'd rather we can go down to the bank and I'll pay you in cash."' Cash Driveway could announce that World War III had commenced but say it in such a way that anyone hearing it would think that everything was going to work out just fine.

James was amazed by this conversation, but at the same time he was amazed that he was amazed. These were the kinds of things that his friend did. This was 100 per cent classic Cash Driveway.

'So what did the guy say?'

'Not much,' said Cash. 'He seemed a little freaked out. But in the end he told me that it was too late. So I had to pay them the money and I have to move out by the end of this week.'

'Where are you going to go?' The realisation that he and Cash had slowly and unintentionally become best friends very much surprised James. And now the idea that his friend could be taken away flattened him like a large man in a leotard jumping off the top rope of a wrestling ring. With everything changing so quickly – his mother dying, meeting Sophie, all the stuff they were doing at the Peggy Day Home – the idea of losing Cash was quite simply unacceptable.

'I have a big place. I've got a spare room. You're moving into my flat. This is not a discussion. The decision has been made,' said James.

'Will you remind me to pay the rent?' asked Cash with a smile that said a thousand thank yous.

'Yes, of course.'

'Well,' said Cash Driveway, 'that, my friend, sounds like a plan.'

Watching Cash's expression change from lost to found, from evicted to invited, felt to James not like he was giving but rather that he was gaining.

And the next day, Cash was living at James' place.

(That was the unexpected thing I told you about.)

Hey! Relax! How many times do I have to tell you that Cash Driveway is not some kind of maniac? He is an artist and has an artistic temperament, that's all. Cash does a hell of a lot more than just smoke dope. He paints. He lectures. He gives away clothes and possessions and money to people who need those things. Cash is a good guy. He is kind, he is smart, he is empathetic and he loves animals. Charlie Girl was one of his best friends. Seriously, Cash Driveway moving in to James' apartment is not going to become a problem in this story.

I think you may be on to me, but let's crack on.

Something that I, your narrator, only found out about years later when talking to Sophie was 'the curse of sundown'. Each day towards early evening at the Peggy Day Home, something quite heartbreaking would occur. At around five or six p.m. many of the women would start fidgeting, fussing about and getting quite anxious. As though there was something that they should be doing. Something quite important and yet something that remained just out of sight, shrouded in the fog of memory. You see, it was dinnertime. The time when, for most of their lives, they had prepared the evening meal for their loved ones. And now that the simple function of providing that had been taken away from them, a strange kind of free-form frustration would descend. An almost audible tension, like a low-level hum, would rise among the patients.

The staff at the home had various ways of dealing with this. One of their preferred methods was for an orderly to tell the patients, 'Tonight we are making you all a special dinner which will be followed by a concert! So, please, everyone, put your feet up and relax. Tonight, let us look after you.' Those patients who were cognisant of the fact that the staff prepared dinner every night, and therefore that it was not actually a special occasion, were also aware that this minor charade was being performed to ease the anxiety and discomfort of some of their fellow patients. That it was a simple kindness. Those lost in their own history, or too far gone to recognise this sleight of hand, were simply pleased that it was happening.

The 'concerts' were almost always performed by Malcolm. He had a good voice, was a confident singer and his guitar playing was sublime. Malcolm usually began with the classic 'California Dreamin'' by the Mamas & the Papas and often other staff members would join him on backing vocals. Sophie had decided, though, that because James may at some point have to pretend to be the son of one or more of the people in the room, he should never join in. Instead, he would stand at the back silently wishing that he was up on stage. For the sake of everyone concerned it was fortunate that he wasn't. I can tell you from personal experience that, for all of his good points, James Rogers has one of the worst singing voices in the southern hemisphere.

There would usually come a time in each concert when people would start calling out requests:

'Play "Lili Marlene"!' 'We want Vivaldi!' There were also occasional demands for more rocking tracks – 'Do "Sympathy for the Devil"' – but not often.

Most of the requests were from a much earlier time. A time that Malcolm had little knowledge of and even less interest in. His response to these requests was almost always the same. When someone excitedly called out for him to play 'I Do Like To Be Beside the Seaside', he would reply: 'I don't know that one, but I can play Neil Young's "Rockin' in the Free World".'

And every time, the crowd would love it.

Sophie would often hear one or other of the women saying something along the lines of 'Oh, dinner and a concert. It's like Mother's Day.'

Sophie would softly smile to herself. 'Yes, *it is* just like Mother's Day. And so it should be.'

One woman seemed to feel the curse of sundown worse than anyone else. Her name was Charlotte Durham, a kind and nervous woman of eighty-five. She had suffered two heart attacks and Alzheimer's was now displacing her memories like an overflowing bath, but she still had occasional moments of gentle clarity. She liked to paint deep and rich still lifes and did so most afternoons; her skill had won her prizes in another time. She could now only paint things that were directly in front of her because everything else was slipping away, but her paintings were beautiful and some hung on the walls of the centre. Charlotte had been a wife and mother and when she was lucid her default setting appeared to be the care and nurture of others – she was often offering to help the staff with whatever work they were doing and was always inquiring as to people's welfare. James imagined her to be a woman who at one point would have approached life with a smiling ease, but whose brow had become steadily more furrowed with confusion the closer she got to what ultimately awaits us all.

Sophie and James decided that Charlotte should be the next person to experience a visit from her 'son'. Numerous times she had mentioned to Sophie that her son Billy was a chef and that every couple of weeks or so he would come to her house and cook her an amazing dinner, and that she was expecting Billy to come by 'any day now'.

Billy had been a chef at DiVada, a famous restaurant in St Kilda. Sophie took a chance and rang the restaurant's owner, Johnny DiVada, and after briefly explaining her connection to Charlotte, she asked him what kind of person Billy had been. According to Johnny DiVada, Billy had not only been an excellent chef; he had also been beloved by his co-workers and his customers, and a very dear friend of Johnny's. But Billy also had his demons (don't we all). He had a low-level heroin habit that he had maintained for a number of years. His drug use had never affected his ability to be a good person or a talented and innovative chef, but it did one day unexpectedly kill him.

It seemed that once Charlotte Durham heard about the death of her son, she had gone downhill very quickly. She was in complete denial about Billy's death, and with her mental and physical health failing rapidly she was moved into the Peggy Day Aged Care Home, where she would tell Sophie Glass about a wonderful son and how any day now he would be coming to cook her dinner.

Hi. How's it all going? As your narrator, I think part of my job should be checking in on you, the reader, every so often, just to see if you are all right. In my opinion, too many narrators try to hide. They try to keep themselves robotic and strictly functional, taking care not to become a part of what is going down. I say, if we are here and you know we are here, we might as well check in from time to time, make sure everybody is comfortable, that everybody has a drink. That everyone has a piece of toast. In fact, if I was you, I would get up right now and make myself some toast, and then come back and read a bit more as I ate.

'But what if I get Vegemite on the clean pages of the book?'

What if you do? I say, damn the torpedoes, go for it. Sometimes it's the risk of Vegemite stains that gives life meaning.

When Sophie told him what she and James were planning for Charlotte Durham, Johnny DiVada was thrilled and offered to provide them with whatever food they needed, cooked by him personally to Billy's recipes. Sophie told James about her conversation with Johnny, and it was all systems go. James' only real objection to the plan was that, as a good cook himself, he didn't want to source the food from DiVada's; he wanted a chance to show off what he could do in the kitchen.

'We don't need to get the food from a restaurant! I've got mad food skills. I'm like a thin, Anglo George Calombaris.'

'Really? Can you cook high-end, innovative Italian food?'

'I can make beef ragout,' replied a dejected James.

'Yes, James, but do you know how to stuff a zucchini flower with crab meat and fennel?'

'Stuff a what?'

'Exactly,' said Sophie. 'We are going to go with Johnny cooking Billy's recipes. But look, apparently Billy's thing was to serve very small courses, and lots of them. Make your beef ragout by all means, and I'll ask Johnny if we can shoehorn it in between a couple of really excellent dishes. Okay? And make sure it's good.'

'Of course it will be good. I'm a really good cook!'

'Yeah?' said Sophie. 'So you keep saying. Currently I only have your word for that.'

'Well, it's true. Come over to my place for dinner one night and find out for yourself,' said James defensively.

'Okay, I will,' replied an equally tetchy Sophie.

'Good,' said James.

'When?'

'How about tomorrow night?'

'Fine!'

Suddenly, they were both smiling.

Hi, it's me again. Sometimes when we plant a seed, nothing happens. No matter how much we water it, no matter how green our thumb – sometimes the seed and the earth and water and sun all get together and say, 'You know what? Fuck it. We're going to have the day off.' If we as humans have learned anything from our time on this planet (and I'm not suggesting that we have) it's that trying to force nature to do things is a pretty dumb idea. Reap the whirlwind, etc. I'm not a scientist but I reckon that nature is massive, and by now, surely, it must be pretty fucked off with humans trying to tell it what to do. Maybe sometimes things are just not meant to grow until they want to.

But other times, you plant a seed and it grows crazy beautiful. It grows bigger, it grows faster, it grows more colourful and more alive than you could ever have imagined. Fortunately and thrillingly for Sophie and James, this is the way that Charlotte Durham's seed grew.

The next day, as James didn't have to go in to the Peggy Day centre, he spent the day preparing for his and Sophie's first official date. At about midday he rode his bike to the Prahran market to buy all of the ingredients he would need for what he hoped would be an impressive meal. James loved the sensory overload that came with big markets. The smells, the sights, the sounds, the tastes. As a twenty-year-old studying art history he had travelled to Europe, where he spent more time in food markets than he did in galleries. When his friends went to the Louvre, James went to the north of France to visit the biggest cheese market he'd ever seen. Instead of focusing on the great museums of London, James went to Soho and hung out at his favourite market, Neal's Yard. While others soaked up the culture of Francis Bacon, James soaked up the culture of actual bacon and unfeasibly large wheels of Jarlsberg. Although he had been raised in a house where the Bible was considered, if at all, as fiction, and as an adult he had remained happily agnostic and blissfully ignorant of organised religions, he supposed that what he experienced in markets was probably what other people experienced in churches. He could drink the wine and eat the flesh without having to feel the guilt of imagining that they belonged to a man on a cross who had already suffered far too much for the ungrateful masses.

To be honest, though, I think I might be crapping on a bit here. I mean, James told me some of this stuff, but I'm probably exaggerating a fair bit with the rest.

Hey, relax, champ. This is a book, not real life. It is allowed to be over-the-top.

James had thought a lot about the dinner he would make for Sophie. James thought a lot about Sophie generally so I guess that kind of makes sense.

The first course, as James had planned it, was to be oysters with a citrus vinaigrette. James was good with vinaigrettes. The main course would be fish cooked in chilli and soy – while it wasn't a dish that was about to win him any awards for originality, everyone who ever tried it had enjoyed it. It was a safe bet.

In between these two courses he'd planned to serve a tom yum soup. When Sophie and James' argument about what to feed Charlotte Durham had miraculously turned into them planning their first date, James had asked Sophie if there was anything in particular that she would like to eat, and she'd mentioned how much she loved tom yum.

It wasn't until he was halfway home on the tram, smiling with pride and anticipation, that James realised while he too loved tom yum soup and had always intended to make it himself, he had never actually got around to it.

'That's cool,' thought James as he got off at his stop, 'I can make tom yum soup. How hard can it be?'

Pretty fucking hard, as it would turn out. Pretty fucking hard.

When James was at the market, despairing over what ingredients to buy for the soup, he called Cash Driveway.

'Hello, James.'

'Hi, Cash. You sound like you've been running.'

'I have,' said Cash. 'I've been running away from something.'

'Interesting,' said James. 'Listen, do you happen to know a recipe for tom yum soup?'

'Yes, I do,' said Cash and then added, 'Do I sound burned?'

'What?'

'Do I sound as though I have recently lost most of my hair in a fire?'

'No,' said James, puzzled. 'You sound reliably hirsute.'

'I hate to disappoint you, but we here at Driveway Industries have just suffered a catastrophe. Do you remember that fully operational petrol-powered car that I was building out of matchsticks? It just burned itself to the ground and exploded.'

'Cash! Was anybody hurt?'

'Artists are always being hurt, James. It comes with the territory. It burned all the grass from the front of my studio and exactly half of the hair from my head. Now, what's this about soup?'

'Sophie is coming over tonight. And I am making her dinner. But I told her that I can make tom yum soup and I can't. I need you to make some for me.'

'I can't make tom yum soup!'

'But you just told me that you could!'

'No, I didn't,' said Cash Driveway. 'I told you that I knew a recipe. The recipe is: go to Thai-tanic and have Graham make you two bowls of it.'

James took Cash's advice. On the way back from the market he stopped at Thai-tanic. Graham was behind the counter chopping chillies with what seemed to James to be a threateningly large cleaver of some kind. As it was four p.m. there was no one else in the restaurant.

'Hey, Graham,' said James, feeling intimidated as he always did when addressing the chef and owner of Thai-Tanic. He wasn't exactly sure why he felt intimidated; it may have been that every time he entered the restaurant Graham was wielding some kind of enormous cooking implement that could easily have been a weapon. Despite this, he'd only ever really had one confrontation with Graham and that was about a year ago. James had said to Graham, 'Man, you make the best beef rendang I've ever had – but rendang is Malaysian, and you run a Thai restaurant. Are you secretly Malaysian?'

Graham went off his head. '*What!* Malaysian? I'm not Malaysian! I'm fifth-generation Thai. I can cook beef rendang because I'm a good chef. You should be very careful who you start calling Malaysian!' he said, waving a large knife dangerously close to James' face. 'I mean, look at my name – *Graham*. Have you ever met a Malaysian person called Graham? No, you haven't, because Graham is a Thai name.'

Since this awkward interaction, they had got along fine. James never mentioned Malaysia again and Graham did his best to ignore the perceived insult.

The day that James was having Sophie over for dinner, Graham looked up as James entered and greeted him. 'James, my friend, one beef rendang to take away?'

'Not today, Graham. Today I want two serves of tom yum chicken soup.'

'Wow,' said Graham. 'That's a double surprise. No beef rendang, and you're ordering *two* things. That implies two people. Is one a lady?'

'Well, yes . . .' said James, blushing.

'Ha!' said Graham. 'And you like her! Your face has gone as red as a beep.'

'As a what?' asked James.

'As a beep – a beeproot.'

'Do you mean beetroot?' asked James, puzzled.

'Hey!' Graham was getting scary. 'I'm the chef. It's *beeproot!*'

'Okay,' said James, feeling intimidated. 'In any case, yes. I like her.'

'All right. Two bowls of tom yum coming up. Give me ten minutes.'

James did what he was told.

When the soup was ready, Graham called James over to the counter. 'There you go. Chicken tom yum, and it is really fucking good.'

'I'm sure it is,' said James. 'Everything you make is good.'

'Are you going to tell her that you made it?'

James felt like he'd been slapped in the face. 'What? Why would I do that?'

'It's just a thing,' said Graham. 'People do it. Especially with soup. It's a kind of human failing.'

'Well, *I'm* not going to . . .' James saw Graham picking up one of his large cleavers. '*Okay!*' he said much louder than he intended. 'Yes! I'm going to tell her that I made it. But only because it's so good and I want her to like me!'

Graham mulled this over for a second before replying, 'Yeah, what the fuck. Why not. I guess it's a kind of compliment.' James' relief was palpable; he exhaled so much that he felt he lost weight.

'Okay,' said Graham. 'That will be twenty-four dollars.'

'It's usually nine dollars a bowl! That makes it eighteen dollars.'

'It's eighteen dollars for people who don't pretend to have made it themselves. The extra six dollars goes into my honesty box,' Graham explained calmly.

'Where is your honesty box?' asked James.

'In my pocket,' said Graham. 'Enjoy your soup, James.'

'I will,' he said as he turned to leave.

'It smells great,' Graham smiled. 'One day you'll have to give me the recipe.'

'Yeah,' said James sheepishly as he walked out the door. 'I might just do that.'

As he left Thai-Tanic, it occurred to James that he couldn't remember the last time that something normal had happened in his life.

And, to his surprise, he didn't really care.

When James got home he decanted the soup into a saucepan and got rid of all the evidence, forcing the takeaway bag and the containers deep into the rubbish bin. He spent the next hour and a half preparing the rest of the meal and tidying up the flat. When I say 'tidying up', I mean more 'moving things around', and when I say 'moving things around', I mean more 'opening the door to Cash's room and throwing everything non-essential in there'. Cash was going out for the night, to a 'marijuana smokers against the patriarchy' lecture. So it was just going to be James and Sophie. The two of them. Together. Alone.

Finally, with everything just about ready, James went into his bedroom to get dressed. He put on a clean pair of jeans, a collared purple shirt and a grey jacket. He stood in front of the mirror before turning to the photo of Charlie Girl and asking, 'What do think, pup?'

He looked good, and if Charlie Girl had actually been there and been able to speak English, she would have told him so.

'Yeah, you're right, I look like an idiot.'

He dumped that look and went for something more casual, a simple light-blue T-shirt under the jacket. At one point while looking into the mirror he tried pulling the sleeves of the jacket up to his elbows. He looked like a low-level drug dealer from an episode of *Miami Vice*.

'How about this?'

If a photograph of a dog with a ball in its mouth could have uttered the words 'Don Johnson', Charlie Girl certainly would have.

In the end he compromised. He wore the T-shirt with the purple shirt over it, unbuttoned. He wanted to look casual, like he didn't care. He wasn't. He did.

Five minutes after he finished dressing the buzzer in his flat went off.

James had no idea that it had taken Sophie numerous glances at her reflection in the downstairs window, a few adjustments to her hair and six false starts before she finally gathered the courage to press the buzzer marked 'James Rogers. Unit 6'.

Ain't love grand?

Sophie handed James a bottle of wine and then picked up the photo of Charlie Girl (which James had strategically placed on view) and said, 'Oh my god! Is this Charlie? She is too beautiful.' That was a good sign. 'Love my dog, love me,' thought James, brazenly inverting a T-shirt slogan.

Their first date went just like most people's first dates go.

(If most people lived in the 1940s and were saving themselves for marriage. Sophie and James were not doing either of those things but, while both of them considered themselves to be smart, savvy and urbane, they were also terrified of saying too much. So instead, as people had for centuries, they just had dinner and said too little.)

They laughed and plotted and talked about Charlotte Durham and their upcoming performance. Working together meant that when a silence grew too long or a gaze too intense, they could safely and annoyingly fall into talking about the Peggy Day centre. But it was a good night – the food was a hit and Sophie had to admit that James could cook. He had worried that he'd put too much chilli and soy in the fish; apparently he hadn't.

'That fish was amazing,' said Sophie. 'I adore chilli and soy.'

'I didn't wreck it by adding the fish, did I?' he replied. 'I could have just served chilli and soy sauce for the main.'

'No, it was perfect. I don't often say this, but I loved it all.' By now James found himself smiling at almost everything she said, and her loving his cooking made him smile a lot.

She particularly liked the tom yum soup and as she never directly asked him how or even *if* he had made it, James didn't feel too bad about his culinary deception. One day he would tell her the whole truth but at that time, in that place, there was too much riding on it.

'What do your parents do? Have you got parents?' James asked Sophie as they walked out onto the balcony with their glasses of wine. It occurred to him that for all of his interest in Sophie, he knew very little about her past.

'I've got a mum,' she replied. 'My father left when I was a kid; I haven't seen him since I was ten. He lives in America, I think.'

'Oh, I'm sorry,' said James with a genuine sense of sorrow for his friend.

'Don't be. Everyone is always sorry. He was a flake. But my mum is fantastic.'

'Great,' said James. 'I never really thought much about my mum while she was alive, and that's because I simply assumed that she would always be around. Now that she's gone I spend heaps of time wondering how I could have made her feel more appreciated.'

'No, Mum and I are pretty good with that stuff. And she loves the fact that I work in aged care. She's sixty-five, in very good health, and absolutely hanging out to move into the Peggy Day. Most people that I know struggle to convince their parents that moving into a retirement village is a good idea. My mother, on the other hand, is absolutely champing at the bit to get in there. I'm sure when that day comes she will completely take the place over.'

'Yeah, go easy,' said James, pretending to be pissed off.

'What?'

'Stop boasting,' he said.

'What are you talking about?'

James was smiling but trying not to.

'You, with your fun stories about your family. "Oh, both my parents are still alive, blah blah blah . . . My mum loves me." Jesus, Soph. Both of my parents are dead. You're being very insensitive.'

'Be quiet, orphan,' she said warmly, pouring them each another glass of wine. She passed him his glass with a smile that lit up the balcony. Then again she also flicked on the light switch at that moment. So it could have been the light that lit up the balcony, I'm not too sure.

Eventually Sophie called an Uber as they had a big day coming up. James opened the apartment door for her and they came together for a peck that hardly qualified as a kiss but, still, it was contact.

After James shut the door they both leaned against opposite sides of the same wall and sighed like frustrated but happy idiots. Sophie said, 'Oh god!', smiled and shook her head nineteen times in the Uber on her way home.

When James eventually went to bed, glaringly alone, he replaced the photo on the mantle. 'I know, Charlie Girl, I know. But other than that, it went pretty well! She loved you. And she liked my, and Graham's, food . . . Glass half full, my licky friend. Glass half full.' And with that he turned off the lights, flopped down on his too-big-for-one-person, bought-for-a-couple, memory-foam-clad, king-sized bed and went to sleep.

Trust me. They are definitely going to have sex. I'm not holding off on that for 'literary suspense' reasons; this is just how it went down. They were both actually that terrified and dumb. Cute, sure, but terrified and dumb. Factaroo, my friends, factaroo.

James and Sophie had put more work, research and thought into their plan for Charlotte Durham than they had for their other attempts, and it showed. This wasn't just going to be James swanning into somebody's room and announcing, 'Hi, I'm your son.' This was going to be a production of Hollywood proportions. James looked the part. He was even wearing a jacket exactly the same as the one Billy was wearing in the photo that Johnny had given them. Sophie had 'set dressed' Charlotte Durham's room with beautiful flowers and candles while Charlotte was at the other end of the complex for her weekly medical check-up. Meanwhile, Malcolm, wearing a suit and tie, had set himself up in the corner of the room and was playing the cello. (I know, right?) When Charlotte came into the room Malcolm would begin playing Trio in E-flat by Franz Schubert. Malcolm generally preferred the

Velvet Underground to Schubert, but it was a genuinely beautiful piece of music. All in all, it was to be a rarified moment. Everyone was at their best, and so was the food.

Johnny DiVada had brought the dishes in on beautiful trays, covered by ornate silver cloches to keep it all hot. Everything was sublime, and James felt very relieved that he hadn't made his beef ragout. It was good, sure, but it wasn't at this level. It would have come in a Tupperware container and he would've felt like a dick.

I'm not going to tell you what the courses of the meal actually were. You would become green with envy. You would put down this book and head immediately to Johnny DiVada's restaurant, calling on the way to make a reservation. When you got there you would say, 'I want Billy's food! The food you made for Charlotte Durham!' And Johnny DiVada would say, 'I have absolutely no idea what you're talking about.' Not because he's cruel or secretive, but because he would literally have absolutely no idea what you were talking about. Let's not forget this is a novel.

Sophie went out into the hallway to take Charlotte Durham and her wheelchair from the orderly who had brought her back from the medical centre.

James went and stood by the window.

Johnny got ready to serve the food.

Malcolm started playing Schubert.

The door opened and there she was.

Charlotte Durham slowly took in the scene. Then her face lit up and she clasped her hands together like a little girl.

'Oh, hello Billy! Hello Johnny! This is just beautiful! What are you boys up to?'

Charlotte's complete and immediate acceptance of the scene being played out in front of and all around her was a joy to behold. It emboldened James, who in no time began finishing his 'mother's' sentences and, brazenly but lovingly, correcting her on certain details of her stories.

'Yes, Mum, I do remember that,' he said. 'But you said that car was green. I seem to remember it was blue. Wasn't it? A blue car?'

At this point Sophie and Johnny exchanged looks that said, 'Oh god, he's losing it.' James' correction of Charlotte even caused the unflappable Malcolm to hit a couple of bum notes.

But James was on a roll. He was in his element. To the astonishment and relief of everyone present, he was exuding such confidence and showing such love that, after the briefest of pauses, Charlotte simply agreed with her 'son'.

'You know, Billy, you just might be right. I think it was a blue car after all.'

As Johnny served everyone's meals he and Charlotte talked about his restaurant and she joked about Billy, teasing him gently, the way that a mother does. Sophie helped Charlotte with her food, cutting it for her, adding sauces and generally making sure that everything was easy and within her reach. Charlotte appreciated and was proud of her son's cooking, but ate very little. Anything she didn't finish (which was everything) she insisted that Sophie give to Malcolm, who sat happily in the corner, between tunes, scoffing course after course.

Once the meal was finished, Charlotte was helped into bed by the four of them. Everybody wanted to be involved. Johnny was straightening her doona, Malcolm fluffing her pillows. Sophie and James eased her back and helped to lay her down. Within seconds of her head touching the pillow, she was blissfully asleep, dreaming of distant times, happy families and blue, blue cars.

The four conspirators made a beeline for the office. The excitement and accomplishment that they felt was way too intense to be displayed in the corridors of an old people's home. It required jumping. It demanded victorious shouting. And anyway, it's hard for four people to give each other hugs and exchange high fives when they are carrying a cello and large silver serving trays.

Once the office door was closed behind them Sophie, James, Malcolm and Johnny went off like a Dutch cracker factory. (A saying I heard a friend use once. I have no idea of its literal meaning but its intention and rhythm are clear enough.) They were like a band who had just played their first really big gig, and played better than they ever had before. They yelled. They hugged. They body slammed. Sophie was so excited that she punched James on the shoulder, as hard as she could. James was so excited that his reaction to this assault was simply to yell 'YES!' three times. Malcolm was having some kind of evangelical experience. Johnny was repeatedly miming kicking a football, before running to the other end of the room and giving himself the all-clear for a goal.

The next morning James dropped in to the Peggy Day Home for a meeting with Sophie to work out who would be next on their list. He chained up his bicycle and ran up the main stairs of the centre, the same stairs he had run up weeks earlier when he had been ninety-three minutes late to see his actual mother.

When he entered the office Sophie was behind the desk beaming. 'Hello, beautiful man,' she said.

'Beautiful man?' replied James, a smile taking over his face. 'You have never been so complimentary. What have I done to deserve that?'

'Everything. This. Our plan. You were amazing yesterday. You were, as described, a beautiful man.'

Looking back later James realised that was the moment that any resistance he had to Sophie, and by then he probably didn't really have much, melted away. That was his Waterloo. To him she was pirate radio and desert treks. She was midnight graffiti runs and ordering things in restaurants because the idea of them terrified you. He was going all in, and hoping for a pair.

'What have you been doing today?' asked Sophie.

'Not much. Cash and I are going out for dinner tonight and we both want you to come.'

'Excellent!' she replied, with an energy that surprised James.

'Why excellent?'

'Because I get to spend time with the enigma that is Cash Driveway.'

'Ha! Be careful what you wish for.'

For a couple of seconds they both stared out the window, watching Mrs Murphy standing next to the oak tree.

Sophie broke the silence. 'So . . .'

'So,' replied James. 'Who's our next parent? Glass–Rogers Enterprises are on a roll.'

'I have a couple of suggestions,' replied Sophie. 'I just thought I'd see what you —'

There was a knock on the door. It opened and Malcolm entered the room. He looked confused. As though he had just been told something that made no sense. He closed the door behind him and leaned against it, as if trying to keep something out.

'Malcolm! King of the cello!' blurted James, unaware of the strange energy that Malcolm had brought into the room.

'Malcolm? Are you okay?' asked Sophie. The look on her face said that she knew he wasn't. Something bad was about to happen.

'It's . . . It's Charlotte Durham . . . She died.' The colour had drained from Malcolm's face.

'What? When?' asked Sophie.

'She didn't wake up this morning . . . I found her . . .' His voice made him sound lost. He was.

'Oh Malcolm,' said Sophie, crossing to him and giving him a hug. 'I'm so sorry.'

Then she tried to take charge. 'It's okay. It's okay. She was eighty-five years old . . . She had lived . . . And yesterday!' Sophie wasn't going to let what they had all done together be washed away with this sadness.

James felt numb. He was staring at Malcolm as though waiting for him to say he was kidding, but he knew that wasn't going to happen. 'We gave her a great afternoon,' he said, looking for the light in this sudden gloom.

'Her last day was pretty cool,' added Malcolm, his face brightening. 'There was a lot of love in that room.'

'There was,' agreed James.

The three friends came together in the middle of the room. The smallest of huddles by a team just realising that, no matter how well they played, they were sometimes going to lose the match.

'Get ready,' said Sophie. 'This is just the beginning . . .'

James and Malcolm understood what she meant and realised that she was completely right. No matter how happy they made the clients. No matter how good a job they did. Whatever food they served, whatever music they played. Death was the inevitable outcome. Sick people sometimes get well, but old people never get younger.

*

James had rung ahead and told Cash what had happened with Charlotte Durham. When Sophie and James arrived at the apartment, Cash opened the door for them and handed them each a glass of wine.

'Hey, James. Hi Sophie, I'm Cash. I'm so sorry for your loss.'

Before she even knew what was happening, tears poured from Sophie's eyes, and she fell into the kind embrace of a man she had only just met. Cash, whatever other qualities he may have possessed, could be a remarkably reassuring man. He held the weeping and exhausted Sophie, stroking her hair. James watched his old friend easing Sophie's heartache and when he met Cash's gaze he saw in those eyes such a deep reservoir of kindness that it brought a lump to his throat. That combined with the fact that the two people he loved the most in the world were embracing in his living room caused James' eyes to unexpectedly fill with tears as well.

The night was, for James and Sophie, something like coming up for air. It was light and fresh and full of hope. This was in no small part due to Cash Driveway's quixotic tales of adventure and, to a lesser extent, his seemingly endless supply of marijuana. It was a beautiful, clear evening that had James and Sophie feeling very glad to be alive.

No. Not that night. Not yet. Seriously, stop asking.

Two days later Sophie had an appointment with a woman named Catherine Darling who had called making inquiries about moving her mother into the Peggy Day Home. As they sat across from one another, Sophie studied Catherine Darling. She was in her mid forties, tall, very attractive, expensively dressed, and had the breezy, confident charm often displayed by minor members of royalty or those who've grown up around serious wealth. Catherine Darling placed her bag on the desk that separated her from Sophie, and began.

'Thank you so much for agreeing to see me.'

'Of course,' replied Sophie.

'It's just that everything is happening so fast, and I really don't know what I should be doing. It's my mother. She's in her late seventies, and she lives alone. She's had a wonderful and independent life, done everything she ever wanted to do, but in the last few years everything has started to fall apart . . . For the last eighteen months or so I've had live-in carers staying with her but that is no longer working. Aside from the fact that she keeps sacking them or driving them away, her staying in the house has become untenable. She needs somewhere with professionals on call 24/7.'

'We really are a great option for when people can no longer take care of themselves. It kind of gives everyone peace of mind,' Sophie agreed.

'Wonderful. And please don't misunderstand me; I've been looking after her for the best part of the last ten years but I have my own family, and work . . .'

'Of course. What do you do?' asked Sophie. 'For work?'

'I run a gallery in the city,' replied Catherine Darling. 'I'm also on a few charity boards, so time is becoming increasingly hard to find.'

'I completely understand. Could you tell me what your mother's physical ailments are?'

'Yes. Yes, I can. They are numerous. She is legally blind. She can no longer walk and is confined to a wheelchair. She has severe arthritis. She has had two strokes and three cancer diagnoses, all of which she has successfully fought. She takes a small pharmacy full of tablets each day; I don't even know what most of them are for. For the last few years she's been getting more and more forgetful, but now that seems to have accelerated to the point where she is getting delusional. Sometimes I can tell she doesn't even know who I am . . .'

At that point Catherine's eyes filled with tears and she let out a tortured sob. She then very quickly, and with practised dignity, took a tissue from her bag and dabbed once at each eye and, in an act of will, dragged herself back from the edge of human emotion.

'I'm sorry about that,' she said as she regained control. 'I love her and I worry about her. Sometimes it all just gets a little too much.'

'Oh please, don't apologise. You're in a safe place. Be as emotional as you need to be.'

Catherine Darling, now fully recovered, was looking at Sophie as though she was speaking a foreign language. Emotional outbursts were, to Catherine, things to be avoided, and on the odd occasion that they were indulged in they were to be forgotten about, quickly. Sophie, blissfully unaware of any of this, just barrelled on:

'You can even smash something if you want to. I do sometimes. It helps. And most of the stuff in here is just cheap junk . . .'

'I'll be fine, but thank you,' said Catherine Darling crisply.

Sophie suddenly felt the need to get the conversation back on track, away from petty vandalism and back onto aged care.

'Look, I can assure you that if your mother comes to stay with us she will be cared for, she will be treated with dignity and she will have access to the best of all professional care. We really would look after her.'

'Well, that sounds ideal,' said Catherine and then after a long pause added, 'Do you have anyone here who could convince her of that?'

'I'm sorry? Convince her?'

'Yes. She is most definitely going to take some convincing. She seems to think that everything is fine. She rolls around blindly in that big house in complete denial of her physical and mental situation. I've lost track of the number of conversations we have had where I have expressed my desire, and my practical need, that she move into some kind of assisted-living situation.'

'And what does she say?' asked Sophie.

'She dismisses it out of hand. She seems to think that she will live forever and that she can do everything by herself. But the truth is, things have to change, and they have to change now.'

'I understand. Of course. But the thing is we generally don't get involved in that side of things. The family usually deals with that and then brings their loved one here. We then show them around and do our best to make them feel safe and appreciated. Is there anyone else that could help? Any other family members?'

'No,' replied Catherine firmly. 'There is only me. My father went years ago. There is no one else. I had a younger brother but he disappeared about twelve years ago. Black sheep of the family – always surrounded himself with very dubious and dangerous people. He went to England and we never heard from him again.'

'Oh, god, I'm so sorry to hear that!' said Sophie.

'No, don't be. It's all just history. My strange family history. But the point is there is no one else; it's just my mother and myself. If there's any way you can help facilitate this, or assist me in convincing her that this is the best place for her to be, I would greatly appreciate it.'

Sophie looked across the desk at Catherine Darling. For all of her obvious education, high-end accessorising and a lifetime of good fortune she was, in that place and at that time, simply another exhausted, desperate woman trying to do what was right by her mother and by herself. Sophie took a deep, calming breath and said, 'There is one thing we could try. Tell me more about your brother . . .'

'You told her fucking what?' James yelled into the phone.

As Sophie had anticipated, her having told Catherine Darling about what they had been doing at the Peggy Day Home was not going down well with James.

'I mean, who is this woman? She could wreck everything! She could have us shut down! Or arrested or something!'

'Relax,' said Sophie. 'You only have to meet her for, like, ten minutes. If you don't feel good about things, we'll leave it. Okay? Tomorrow morning. Ten a.m. Just a meeting.'

'All right,' said James. 'I'll be there. But I'm pretty sure this is how World War II started.'

'I'm pretty sure it isn't,' said Sophie.

*

The next morning James arrived at the centre half an hour earlier than he had to in an attempt to get there before Catherine Darling. Sophie was in her office.

'Please don't be pissed off,' she said as soon as James walked in.

'I'm not,' said James. 'Seriously. Not any more. I was, but then I talked about it with Cash. He thinks it's a great idea. A way for me to show my skills in an away game. I mean, I'll be trying this on in the woman's own house! That's pretty out there . . . What do you know about the son?'

'Not much. His name was Robert and he disappeared about twelve years ago in mysterious circumstances in the UK.'

'See? This sounds awesome!' said James.

'Just keep it together, champ. You haven't even met the woman yet.'

'Did you just "champ" me?' he asked.

'Did I what?'

'Did you just "champ" me? It's a thing. Sometimes you can call someone champ just because they're a champ. But sometimes you can call someone champ if you're trying to patronise them or make them see that they're behaving like an idiot.'

'Well, in that case,' said Sophie, 'yes. I definitely just champed you.'

A short while later Catherine Darling was shown into the office by a member of staff.

'Good morning,' said Sophie, 'Catherine Darling, this is James Rogers.'

'So, you are the master of disguise?' said Catherine archly as the three of them sat down.

'Oh well, that may be exaggerating my skill set slightly,' said James. 'To be honest it's more just us going for a rough physical resemblance and then hoping that the old people are blind enough and out of it enough not to notice the difference . . . Sorry, I'm making it sound kind of shitty.'

'No, not at all,' said Catherine Darling. 'And it just so happens that my mother is both "blind enough and out of it enough" to go for this. The fact that your body shape and size are roughly the same as Robert's is a convenient coincidence. I honestly see this working. All you have to do is convince her to move in.'

'Can you tell us a bit about Robert?' asked James.

'Of course. Robert was my only sibling. My younger brother; he would now be forty-one years old. A few years older than you, by the looks of things, but I don't think that will be a problem.'

'What happened to him?' asked James.

'No one really knows. Or more correctly, *someone* definitely knows, but we don't. Robert was always a little bit drawn to crime. God knows why; he certainly didn't need the money. I think it was probably just the thrill he got from being around those kinds of people. He went to the UK and that was the last we ever heard from him. I think he got out of his depth, in over his head, and somebody killed him. The police found his wallet and his passport on the side of the M1.'

'How was your mother with his disappearance?' asked Sophie.

'Well, she never really wanted to know about his dark side. In many ways, he was her favourite. At the time that he went missing she was concerned but I think she always assumed that he would come home. Over time, I guess that became less and less likely. But in the last couple of years, as she has slipped further away from reality, she has started talking about him as though he will be coming home from England any day. I think the best way to go forward is that I will tell her that Robert is indeed coming home, and then I take you, James, as Robert, around to the house as soon as possible. You chat with her, you spend some time with her, and you convince her that it is in her best interests to leave the house and move into the centre,' said Catherine.

'Well, sure. I guess so,' replied James, not entirely happy that someone was muscling in on his one-man show. He wanted to say 'I don't take notes!' in a theatrical voice, but, in a rare case of sound judgement, thought better of it.

'Did you bring the information on your mother?' asked Sophie.

At that Catherine Darling produced a manila folder marked 'Tamara Higginson' and placed it on the desk between James and Sophie.

'I imagine everything is there,' she said. 'If you need to print anything I also have the whole thing on a USB,' she added, dropping a stick on top of the file. 'Listen, I know this is all very short notice, but if you can pull this off, and have "Robert" convince her to move into the centre, you will be doing my family an enormous favour. As such, I would like to do something for you in return. The moment my mother signs the papers and agrees to come live here, I will, on behalf of my family's trust, donate fifty thousand dollars to the Peggy Day Home, to be spent however you see fit.'

Sophie was genuinely shocked. 'Oh no. Catherine, you don't have to do that!'

James was also genuinely shocked by the offer but, unlike Sophie, he was far more ready to run with it. 'When you say to be spent however we see fit —'

'That won't be necessary,' said Sophie, firmly. 'We greatly appreciate the offer but really it's too much.'

'Well, we'll see,' said Catherine as she got up to leave. 'Perhaps we can discuss it another time. I hope everything you need is in the files. If not, feel free to call me at any time. I will ring in the morning and if the two of you are comfortable with everything, I'll take James around to meet my mother in the afternoon. Does that sound like a plan?'

'It certainly does,' said Sophie.

'Yes. We'll see you then,' said James from the desk, still somewhat in shock at the thought of 50 000 of anything, let alone dollars.

After Catherine had left, Sophie and James sat down to go through the file and to talk about what she had suggested.

'What do you think?' asked Sophie.

James looked up from the file. 'Why not? It seems pretty doable.'

'Yeah but . . .'

'But what?' he asked.

'Well, you'll be on your own. I won't be there. What if it goes horribly wrong?'

'It won't. Catherine will be there. She'll back me up. And the fifty thousand dollars . . .'

'We are not taking the fifty thousand dollars. Forget about it.'

'Oh Soph! Why? Think of all the cool things we could spend the money on. Things to make this place rock. Things that the residents need. And then we could spend the rest on wild parties!'

'It's not going to happen, champ.'

'Ouch!'

'So, are you fine with this as it stands?' continued Sophie. 'Just take the file home, learn everything you can about Robert and Tamara, and we'll meet up in the morning.'

James got up to leave. 'No problem. I'm feeling really confident. I think this could be the best one that we've done.'

'Great. Great. I'm glad. If anybody can pull this off, it's you. If you need anything tonight just call me, okay? And James?' He looked back to her. 'You really are a champ. I mean it.'

That night over dinner from Thai-tanic, James told Cash about Catherine and Robert and Tamara Higginson. Cash liked the plan, but then again Cash liked most things except for offal.

'If she says that you don't look like her son,' suggested Cash, 'just tell her that you have been working for the CIA and that they made you get plastic surgery.' If anyone else had suggested this James would have thought they were trying to be funny. But someone else wasn't suggesting it; Cash Driveway was suggesting it, and the look on his face said he was being completely serious.

'Okay,' said James, 'I'll keep that in mind.'

'Did I ever tell you about the time in England when for a day and a half I had a job as Tony Blair's body double?' asked Cash, as though this was the most normal thing in the world.

'What? Tony Blair, the former prime minister?'

'Well, he was the current prime minister then,' replied Cash.

'But you don't look anything like Tony Blair,' said James, baffled.

'I know. I think that's why I only had the job for a day and a half.'

'Why did he even need a body double?' asked James.

'Well, I don't know. I guess in case someone tried to shoot him or something,' said Cash.

'But Cash! That means somebody could have shot you!' James said this assuming that the possibility would not have occurred to Cash.

'Probably not,' said Cash calmly. 'They would've just looked at me through the scope of the sniper rifle and thought, "That's not Tony Blair; that guy looks nothing like him," and then they would've just packed up and gone home.'

James' face had the expression it often had when he was talking to Cash about things like this. Not so much 'is this true?' but more 'how did we end up here?'

Cash picked up Tamara Higginson's folder, studying a photo of her. 'James, she's beautiful. She looks like someone who has lived life on her own terms. Like someone who is rich but isn't an arse- hole. I would very much like to paint Tamara Higginson.'

'Well, old friend, if I work my magic tomorrow and she moves into the Peggy Day Home, I'll ask her if you can come down some- time and set up the easel,' said James.

'Great. Hey, do you know where the word easel comes from, James? It comes from a time when artists would sell their paintings, out in public, as they were painting them. Having them on display as they were being done made for an easier sale. "Easy sale". Thus, "easy sell", thus "easel". That's where the word comes from.'

'Seriously?'

'No. Not at all. That's a ridiculous notion. I just made it up. And with that attempted deception, I'm off to bed.' Cash loved making James believe the unbelievable, and he smiled as he said, 'Goodnight, Mr Rogers.'

'Goodnight, Mr Driveway.'

James sat up for another hour or so reading about Tamara Higginson before going to sleep. I'd tell you what he dreamed of, but, as we all know, other people's dreams are tedious.

The next morning, after a series of phone calls, it was decided that the plan would go ahead; Catherine would pick James up from the Peggy Day Home at eleven.

As she drove, Catherine had a steely focus that had been missing at their first meeting.

'Are you ready for this?' she asked him, her eyes on the street.

'Sure, no problem,' said James.

'Good. You have to come through for me, James. We can't go on like this. I've told her that Robert is back from London and that I'm bringing him over today. When we get there I'll say hi and then leave you two to talk.'

'What, without you there?' said James, a hint of panic in his voice.

'You'll be fine. She's thrilled that you're coming home. And I've told her we can only stay for a little while as I have to take you into the city to see about a job managing a hotel. Just talk with her for an hour or so, have a cup of tea, convince her to move into the centre, and it's job done.'

'You make it sound really easy. It hardly ever is. In fact, the only times it was easy were the first time and the third time,' said James.

'How many times have you done this?' asked Catherine.

'Three.'

'So it has been less than easy one time? All the other times it's been easy?'

'Yeah, I suppose,' said James.

At that point Catherine pulled the Range Rover over. They had been driving through the streets of South Yarra and Toorak. Nice people in a nice car moving through nice suburbs towards deception, however well intentioned. She pulled on the handbrake and turned to him.

'James. It is vital that this happens today. When we leave the house she has to have agreed to move.'

'Well, I'll certainly give it my all,' he said, not really sure where this was going.

'You *have* to,' she said with sudden grimness. 'Look, yesterday when I mentioned donating the fifty thousand dollars, I noticed that you were far more interested in the idea than your girlfriend was.'

'She's not my girlfriend!'

'Whatever. You liked the idea better than Sophie did.'

'Yeah, coveting money is one of my hobbies.'

'Okay. I really need you to get my mother to agree – but it has to be today. If you can get the job done, and I have enormous faith that you can, I will transfer ten thousand dollars into your bank account this afternoon.'

'What!' exclaimed James. The way that Catherine talked about giving away large sums of money so casually was making him nervous. It was making him feel like they were doing something wrong, and that's not what this was. They weren't doing anything wrong; they were doing just the opposite. They were trying to make people feel good. And at least up until then, large sums of money had had nothing to do with it.

'Are you okay with that?' asked Catherine.

'God, yes, I'm okay with it. I'm extremely okay with it. But you don't have to do this.'

'I know I don't have to do it. I'm doing it because I want the job done,' she said as she put the car back into gear. 'Do we have a deal?'

'Yes! Yes, we have a deal.'

And with that Catherine and James drove the last few minutes to the house.

Tamara Higginson lived on one of the better streets in one of Melbourne's better suburbs, Armadale. James had always liked the area, because Armadale, while incredibly beautiful, was not austere or forbidding. Unlike similarly luxurious suburbs, Armadale did not give off a vibe of 'what the fuck are you doing here?'

James was still thinking about the $10 000 as they pulled off the leafy street and into a driveway. The house in front of him was old and stately, and the garden was immaculate.

'Wow,' said James. 'This is pretty cool. Did you grow up in this house?'

'I did,' said Catherine as she turned off the car. 'It was lovely. Are you ready?'

'I guess so,' replied James.

And with that he followed Catherine up the winding, manicured path that led to Tamara Higginson.

Inside, the house was warm and light with high ceilings and
expensive, tasteful furniture. As they walked down the hallway
James noticed the art hanging in various rooms. He saw repro-
ductions of twentieth-century masters, painters he had studied
at art school: Klimt, Picasso, Bacon, Whiteley, Dali, Warhol.
Tamara Higginson, or someone who had lived here, was a fan of
modern art.

Catherine was calling out in a singsong voice, 'Mother, he's
here! Robert's here!' At the end of the hallway was a large open-
plan kitchen with what looked to be a comfortable den off to one
side. It was there that James first saw her. Tamara Higginson was
an old but very impressive woman. Dark glasses covered her eyes
and she moved her head in a way that suggested she was almost
totally blind. James also noticed that she wore two hearing aids.
But what struck James the most on their first meeting was that she
was just sitting there, doing nothing but waiting. Waiting for what?
For him? For something more permanent? 'God,' James thought to
himself, 'getting old really sucks.' He snapped out of it just in time
to hear Catherine saying, 'Look who's here, Mother, it's Robert!'

'Hello, Mum!' he said, reaching a hand out to take hers.
Of course, because she was blind she didn't notice this gesture
and his hand just remained awkwardly suspended in the space
between them.

Fortunately for James, upon hearing 'Robert's' voice, a beautiful smile spread across Tamara's face and she immediately gestured
for him to come and sit on the huge bone-coloured couch that was
next to her wheelchair.

'Oh, Robert, you certainly know how to make an exit. You said you were going for a couple of weeks, but you've been gone for about a hundred years.'

'Well,' replied James, 'it wasn't that long.'

'Catherine, get your brother something to eat. There's plenty in the refrigerator; Posey just came by and stocked it. Get him some ham and cheese and whatnot. Robert, you must be absolutely starving . . .'

'Mum, I have eaten in the last twelve years,' he replied.

'I doubt that. You were never very good at taking care of yourself. There is also some fresh bread in the pantry, Catherine.'

'Yes, Catherine,' said James, 'some fresh bread would be rather nice.'

Catherine was looking at him with the expression of someone who was neither interested in nor experienced at putting things on plates for the sustenance of other people. When she begrudgingly brought him a snack of rather delicious ham, cheese, olives and bread, her manner could best be described as disdainful. She crouched down by her mother and said, 'You two obviously have a lot of catching up to do. I have to head down to High Street and do a couple of things at the Town Hall. Why don't I just leave the two of you alone? I'll be back in about an hour so relax until then.'

The look that she was giving James said anything but 'relax', though. It said 'get this done and get it done quickly'.

'That sounds wonderful, Catherine,' said Tamara.

'I'll walk you out, sis,' said James.

Catherine gave her mother a kiss on the cheek and then James followed her back along the hallway to the front door.

'Where are you going?' he whispered.

'I'm not going anywhere. I just wanted to leave you two together. I will be sitting right out front in the car.'

'What? What if she sees you?' said James, starting to panic a little at Catherine's cavalier attitude.

'She won't see me. Even if she wasn't blind, she's in a wheel-chair – she can't even make it into the front room of the house.' Catherine then placed a hand on his shoulder. 'Look, James, relax. You are good at this, okay?' And then more sternly: 'Just get it done.' With that she left James and Tamara alone. Together for the first time in twelve years, and for the first time ever.

On his return trip down the hallway James took his time. It really was a beautiful house and clearly someone had thought about the design and the decoration of each of the rooms very thoroughly. Nothing, it seemed, had been left to chance.

When he got back to Tamara, he apologised for having taken so long, explaining that he had had to help his sister with something in her car.

'That's all right, Robert. At least you came back this time. I didn't want to wait another twelve years.'

They both smiled.

'Do you want anything while I'm up, Mum?' he asked.

'Yes, Robert. I think I would like a very strong vodka and tonic, to celebrate the return of my prodigal son,' she replied.

'Is that okay? I mean, with the doctors?'

'Vodka is fine, Robert; it's one of my very last pleasures.'

'All right, Mum, I was just checking,' said James. 'To be honest I could murder a vodka. Where is it?'

'Where it has always been,' said Tamara, causing James to have a minor anxiety attack.

'God, it's been a while . . .'

'It's in the pantry next to the refrigerator. You young people have no stamina for memory.'

James wasn't sure if 'stamina for memory' was even a thing, but he certainly liked the way she used words. He made the drinks, handing one to Tamara and rejoining her on the end of the comfortable couch.

They drank and chatted, and James felt, considering the fraud he was perpetuating, remarkably at home in her presence. He wished she would take her large dark glasses off so that he could see more of her face, her eyes. But even with much of her face hidden by the glasses she was an incredibly compelling person to look at. She had the inherent confidence and natural grace of the radically beautiful. And that doesn't go away, not ever.

To James, especially early in their chat, Tamara seemed to alternate between moments of great lucidity when she was sharp and vibrant and periods of foggy confusion in which she would ask the same questions she had already asked, or talk about something that had happened ten years earlier as though it were happening right now.

The first time that James broached the subject of her leaving the house and moving into the Peggy Day Home he felt awkward, but he powered through his spiel driven by the fact that he believed he was right. He explained that both he and Catherine had thought long and hard about it, and they knew, they just knew, that it was the best thing for her to do. He didn't mention that Catherine had offered him 10 000 reasons to feel this way.

After he had finished speaking Tamara sat very still as though taking in everything that he had said, before replying, 'You know, Robert, your father never, in his entire life, ate a meat pie.'

'What?'

'Not ever!' she continued. 'Not even as a child. I once asked him why he had never eaten one, but he changed the subject.'

'Kind of like you just did,' said James.

'Yes. Yes, rather like that,' she said, smiling. 'Now, tell me about your adventures – and get me another vodka.'

This was not going to be easy.

The longer they talked, the more present Tamara seemed to become. After about forty minutes, James thought that he should bring up the topic of her moving into the home again. He found his opening and went for it. When he was about halfway through what was essentially a repeat of his earlier speech, Tamara lifted her drink in his direction and said, 'Stop. Robert, please. Enough. I know, I know. Both you and Catherine make very good and very sensible points. I understand. As my health worsens it's going to become more and more difficult for me to stay here in my house, in our house. I know you only want what's right for me and what you're talking about, me moving into a home, is sadly inevitable.'

James, who had been expecting more resistance, was temporarily stunned.

'So will you do it? Can I tell Catherine that you said yes?' He was close.

'I tell you what. Are you going to be sleeping in your old room?' she asked.

For some reason this simple question made his deception feel all too real.

'Ah, no . . .' said James, slightly thrown. 'I have a hotel in the city, all my stuff is there.'

'Well, can you come back tomorrow?'

'Of course I can. I'm here for you. We both are.' James wondered where this was going.

Tamara continued, 'If you come back at around the same time tomorrow I'll have an answer for you, okay? Now, before you start pushing, I think we both know that I'm going to say yes. But I simply refuse to be pressured into an immediate response; that's Catherine's doing and you can tell her that I know that. She has little to no patience. Come back tomorrow and you'll get your answer. And have I ever been able to say no to you?' She was smiling, which made James smile.

'No, Mum, I guess you haven't. But I better go now, I don't want to miss my job interview. Do you need anything before I go?'

'No, darling, I know where the fridge is and I know how to work the stereo. As long as you put the vodka back in the pantry, I'll be a very happy girl.'

James leaned down and kissed Tamara on the cheek, and she reached up to touch his hair.

'I'll see you tomorrow, Mum.'

As James walked away, he looked back and thought that she looked smaller than she had when he'd first seen her, more frail. He hoped that wasn't because of him.

James pulled the screen door shut behind him and saw Catherine in the Range Rover eyeing him with anticipation. He offered her a noncommittal smile. As he climbed into the car she was immediately on him: 'Well?'

'What an amazing woman,' said James.

'Yes, she's amazing. Did you get her to agree?' asked Catherine impatiently.

'Pretty much . . .'

'Oh James!' cried Catherine in exasperation. 'This has to happen. I told you! It has to happen *today.*'

'Well, Catherine, it's not going to happen today. Okay? She told me that she felt pressured and that you in particular were trying to push her into making a decision. She doesn't like being pushed. I know you think you're doing the right thing, and you are. But you're also asking a proud woman to walk out of her home and leave a lifetime of possessions and experiences and memories. She wants twenty-four hours to think about it. I don't think that's asking too much.'

'I don't care what you think, James,' said Catherine, revealing a hitherto unseen ice-cold side. 'You're a hired gun and nothing more. She's my mother, not yours.'

'I hate to pull you up there, Catherine, but technically she is now *our* mother, and in the interests of achieving your objective, I'd say my opinion matters quite a fucking bit.'

Catherine punched the top of the steering wheel with both of her fists and groaned in frustration before turning to James and, in a conciliatory tone, saying, 'I know, I know. You are right, and whatever you did in there obviously worked. I'm sorry, I'm just so frustrated. This whole thing is equally kind and cruel and it's driving me out of my mind. I do appreciate what you are doing. Just call me tomorrow afternoon once she has agreed. And the ten thousand dollars is still there for you.'

James surprised himself by saying, 'I'm not doing it for the money.'

Catherine looked at her watch suddenly. 'Shit. I'm late! I have to take my daughter to the orthodontist. Can you get a taxi home? And one back here to see her tomorrow?'

'Sure,' said James. 'No problem. I'll get an Uber.'

'Great,' she replied. 'Call me tomorrow afternoon, as soon as it's done. I'll come over and spend some time with you both. Some "family" time.'

'That will be nice – and creepy,' said James.

'Okay, I'll see you then. Good luck.'

Catherine pulled away and out on to the street, leaving James standing on the semicircular driveway, in the ornate and impressive front garden that belonged, at least for the next twenty-four hours, to Tamara Higginson.

James wanted out of there. Although his intentions were good he felt oddly dirty. Why had she offered him the money? Maybe it was just an incentive; maybe it didn't mean anything. But it was making him uneasy. He wasn't doing this for the money, but it isn't easy to say no to $10 000.

He needed to call an Uber, but more importantly he needed to call Sophie. He needed to feel safe and at home, and, more than anyone he knew, Sophie could make him feel both of those things. He held his breath for a moment and then thought, 'Just go for it!'

'Soph, it's me. Hi. The Tamara Higginson thing went okay. I have to come back tomorrow, but it's fine. Now listen, there is something I have to tell you. I'm going to tell it to you and I don't want you to interrupt, okay? Right. I've been thinking about us, about you and me. A lot. All the time in fact. But I haven't known how to tell you what I feel, so . . . so I'm just going to go for it. I love you. I'm in love with you. I have been from the moment that we met and it is only getting stronger all the time. I want to hold you and sleep with you and melt into you . . . The idea of not telling you this has just become unbearable. I want to spend the rest of eternity with you, or at least the next few months. Is there any possible chance that you feel the same way about me?'

James paused for a moment. That was intense. He hadn't actually been speaking to Sophie; he'd just been practising to see how it sounded. Those words quite accurately described how he felt about Sophie, but there was no way he was going to say them to her. Not yet, anyway. Saying those words to himself in the front yard of a stranger's home was fine, but telling Sophie? No way.

But he did want to talk to her, to hear her voice. To tell her about his day and to ask her about her own. He reached for his phone. It wasn't in his back pocket. He tried all his other pockets. It wasn't there.

Then he remembered something. He'd taken his phone out of his pocket and put it next to him while he was talking to Tamara Higginson. He remembered putting it down but he didn't remember picking it up. His phone was inside the house next to where he had been sitting, on Tamara's couch.

He decided that he would let himself back into the house. If Tamara was where he had left her, he would pick up his phone, make his explanation and go. If she wasn't where he had left her, and he couldn't see her anywhere else, he would quickly and quietly move through the house, grab the phone, and split.

He opened the screen door and made his way down the corridor, past the Picasso, past the Warhols, to the den where the two of them had sat.

Suddenly he stopped in his tracks. He was staring at something that was definitely not as it should be. It was Tamara's wheelchair.

And it was empty.

At first he thought something must have gone wrong. That she must have fallen out of the wheelchair and was no doubt lying somewhere nearby, badly hurt. But then he noticed something moving in his peripheral vision. He turned to face Tamara Higginson. Tall and regal, dark glasses off, standing at the kitchen bench making herself a vodka and tonic.

'Mum!' said James, in shock. 'You're . . . You're not paralysed.'

She fixed him with her piercing blue eyes:

'No. No, I'm not. And you are not my fucking son.'

You could have called the situation awkward without being accused of exaggerating.

'What is your name?' demanded Tamara. 'Who are you?'

'My name is James. James Rogers.' He was thinking on his feet but the only thing he was thinking was, 'Oh shit, this is not going the way it was meant to.'

Tamara poured a second vodka tonic, a very strong one, and handed it to him.

'Sit down, James Rogers,' she said. 'You and I are going to have a little talk.'

James did as he was told.

'You know, you look nothing like my son,' said Tamara.

'Right. So you can see?' asked a sheepish James.

'Of course I can see. And even if I couldn't see, I would know you were not my son. My son died in a drug deal gone wrong somewhere outside of Birmingham twelve years ago. He was in many ways a lovely boy, but he was also a complete lunatic. No matter what anyone told him, Robert was going to keep poking the bear with a stick until one day the bear tore him to pieces. Catherine doesn't know that I know this, of course. You might have noticed that we're not the best at communication. Did my daughter hire you, James Rogers?'

'No. Well, yes. But it's not about the money.'

'How much? How much did my terribly concerned daughter offer to pay you to get me out of my house?'

'Ten thousand,' said James, appalled at how honest he was being.

'Ten thousand? I actually thought she would have gone higher.'

'I'm pretty cheap,' said James, before adding, 'Look, I'm not some criminal for hire that she found on Gumtree. I actually work at the Peggy Day Home. I'm not the best person on earth but I'm not the worst either. I'm nowhere near as horrible as I seem right now.'

James then went on to tell Tamara about his mother and the Peggy Day Home, and about Sophie and what they had been doing with the clients. He told her about Malcolm and Johnny (she of course, like everyone, knew Johnny and had dined at his restaurant numerous times). In closing he told her: 'We honestly thought it was a good idea, even though it sounds kind of insane now . . . But please don't go crazy at Catherine; she was only doing what she thought was right. You're her mum and she loves you very much.'

'Oh, James Rogers, don't be fooled by Catherine. My daughter is not who she seems to be.'

'Well, in her defence, none of us are really "who we seem to be" today, are we?' said the artist formerly known as Robert. 'For example, your health seems to have radically improved in the last ten minutes or so.'

'Yes, I've noticed that too,' said the increasingly robust Tamara. 'I feel much better.'

'Your memory?'

'Also vastly improved.'

'Your paraplegia?' he inquired.

'Seems to have eased right off. I probably just needed a bit of a sit down.'

'And your blindness?'

'Cleary temporary,' she said, enjoying herself.

'Why you are doing all of this?' he asked.

'Oh, James Rogers,' smiled Tamara. 'I thought you would never ask. Another vodka?'

She mixed two fresh drinks, sat down with him on the couch and told him some of her story. Her husband, Morgan Higginson, had died suddenly, over twenty years ago. Though it was painful she had adjusted to his absence and carried on. Then twelve years later Robert had disappeared and not long after she'd received evidence of his brutal death. The loss of her child, she explained, was something she had never really come to terms with. For a year or so she had been completely devastated, almost to the point of immobility, and she kept the news to herself, desperately hoping that perhaps if she didn't share it it wouldn't be true. And then eventually, she had begun to regain something resembling her old life. Gently she began socialising, going to exhibitions, lunching with friends, seeing films and plays, doing all of the things that she used to do before fate decided to carve two huge chunks out of her life. It was around this time, just as she was starting to live again, that she noticed a change in her daughter. Catherine became obsessed by the idea that her mother could no longer control her own day-to-day existence – but more importantly, and more tellingly, Catherine became obsessed by the idea that her mother was no longer mentally fit to remain in control of the family's substantial holdings. She had papers drawn up and then came to her mother one day insisting that she sign them, and that she, Catherine, take control of the family's financial interests. Tamara politely refused to do anything of the sort.

Instead, Tamara had made a will, in which she had provided generously for her daughter – or, as she described it to James, 'I left her about fifteen million "in cash and prizes", to use the parlance of a television game show.'

James thought, 'Did she just say fifteen million?'

While Tamara had provided for Catherine, it seemed she hadn't provided enough. Her will stated that her daughter would receive 40 per cent of the family fortune, but Tamara was and always had been a philanthropist, and so the other 60 per cent was to be shared between various charities, arts organisations and animal welfare groups. This didn't please Catherine, who wanted the remaining 60 per cent to be shared between Catherine and Catherine. And thus began what Tamara described as a war of attrition, full of dirty tricks and double crosses. 'Our tactics have occasionally changed,' said Tamara, 'our weapons occasionally change, but the prize remains the same.'

'So am I a weapon?' asked a thoroughly compelled James.

'You were, yes. An ingenious one. Something of a Trojan horse.'

'So why the wheelchair? Why the paralysis and the blindness?' he asked.

'It started out as a misguided appeal to her sense of humanity. Ha! It didn't even slow her down. But the blindness? The blindness was a stroke of genius. I have a wonderful doctor who knows this whole story and is quite complicit with me. He suggested pretending to be blind as just another of my numerous symptoms. But it came with a bonus that neither of us had expected. With me wearing the dark glasses and Catherine accepting that I was blind, she started to physically relax in front of me. From behind my sunglasses I looked at her face, her expressions, her actions, and I could read her like a cheap airport novel.'

'Jesus,' said James 'This is just so . . .'

'I know, James, it is indeed. And the main problem for me now is that all of my contrived ailments haven't made her back off at all. In fact, quite the opposite is true. She senses weakness. She's like a shark with blood in the water.'

'So what are you going to do?' asked James.

Tamara paused for a moment and then looked him in the eyes before replying, 'I guess eventually I will move into care, but I'd like to do it on my terms, not when my ungrateful child decides that I am no longer of use to her. Isn't it fun meeting my family? I bet you are glad you came!'

'I actually am, for some strange reason. I really like you, Mrs Higginson. Can I switch sides? I could be a double agent.'

'You can do whatever you want, James, but if you ever call me Mrs Higginson again, I'll have you killed. We rich people do that all the time.'

'Okay, Tamara. Thanks for the tip.'

Tamara Higginson leaned back into the couch, crossing her legs at the ankles. She reminded James of someone like Charlotte Rampling, Maggie Smith or Bette Davis – some impossibly glamorous movie star from an impossibly glamorous movie.

'James,' she said, 'it has been an absolute thrill to spend time with you, even if both of us were a trifle fraudulent on first meeting. To be able to honestly communicate with someone about what is going on in my life, to be able to take off those ludicrous glasses, to get up out of that ridiculous wheelchair, and to actually talk with someone who at least appeared to be listening – it has given me more than I can even say. You listened to my story, I listened to yours. It's been very egalitarian. Although, of course, my story was more interesting than yours,' she added, straight-faced.

'No way!' interjected James, smiling. 'My life is way more interesting than yours, Tamara. You just haven't heard much about my life yet, primarily because you've been going on and on about yourself: "Oh, poor me, I've got a mean daughter and heaps of cash, blah blah blah".'

She laughed at his nerve.

'I have a fascinating life. I haven't even told you about my friend Cash Driveway yet,' James went on.

'Who?' asked Tamara.

'Exactly. See, you *are* intrigued.'

Tamara Higginson made them both bloody marys and some lovely stuff to munch on, and they continued on like this for the next couple of hours, laughing, listening to music and having a far better time in each other's company than either of them could ever have imagined. At a certain point James decided that it was probably best if he rang Sophie and told her what was going on. He excused himself and went out to the beautifully landscaped backyard. After fumbling through most of what had happened he ended with 'and that is pretty much where things stand'.

'So,' said Sophie, 'it's business as usual then. Everything sounds as though it's going exactly to plan.' She laughed.

'I'm glad you're not pissed off,' said James.

'Pissed off? How could I be? We always knew this wasn't an exact science. And I'm actually really proud of the way you're handling it. I probably would've freaked out in your situation. And Tamara Higginson sounds amazing. Have a bloody mary for me, and keep me informed.'

'Will do, chief,' said James.

'Hey, Tamara Higginson,' said James as he walked back in to the house. 'Can I make you dinner tonight?'

'Why, yes, James Rogers, so long as you can cook.'

'Oh, I can cook,' said James, forgetting about his recent attempt at tom yum soup. 'And I assume you have every ingredient known to man. Is that a rich person thing?'

'It is, James. Access to unlimited ingredients is one of the underestimated bonuses of being wealthy. That and having psychotically greedy children.'

James cooked a zucchini, capsicum and red lentil dhal with rice as they continued chatting. They washed it down with a crisp sav blanc, which left them very happy indeed. After dinner, as Tamara put the plates in the dishwasher and James washed the pans in the sink, she calmly announced: 'Okay, James, I have a plan. I think that it's time Catherine and I made a deal. We are, after all, a family, or what's left of one. I will meet with her and I will tell her the truth. I will also tell her that I will leave this house and move into your place of employment within the next fortnight.'

'That's pretty quick,' said James. 'Are you sure?'

'Yes, I am. I can't be bothered doing this any more. And, while I love this house, it's beginning to feel very big and empty. So I will agree to move – but only on two conditions. She can take the house and the 40 per cent as laid down in my will, but she must drop her claim to everything else. The rest of my money goes exactly where I want it to go. She can either accept that deal or she can watch as I start to spend her inheritance on extremely expensive lawyers. What do you think?'

'It sounds pretty severe, but it also sounds like a really good plan. Obviously I don't know her all that well, but I reckon she'll go for it.'

'So do I,' said Tamara confidently.

James was very much enjoying the company of this remarkable woman. 'What was your other condition? You said you would do this but only on *two* conditions. What was the other one?'

'The other condition, James, is that you and I go on a road trip.'

'We go on a what?' said James.

'You heard. We go on a road trip.'

'A road trip to where? Do you mean to the shops or something?'

This was getting more and more strange by the minute. A couple of hours ago they had been both happily lying to each other, now the woman whose son he had been pretending to be was suggesting that they go on a road trip together. When? How? Where to?

'No, James, I don't. I mean a proper road trip, to Byron Bay. There is someone there that I have to see. After that? I'll happily come and live at your Peggy Day centre and you can pretend to be my son all day long if you want to,' said Tamara.

Tamara sat down next to James on the couch and locked onto him with her steely blue eyes, which made James feel both utterly

calm and completely terrified at the same time. Like a wave breaking in all directions, forward and backwards, fast and slow, all
at once.

Tamara began: 'Can you drive?'

'What? Yes, I can drive,' said James, confused by this abrupt
question.

'Good. We'll be driving. Or rather, *you* will be driving. I have
a beautiful old Jag; you'll love it. Everybody loves it. Listen, James,
I know we've only just met and that the circumstances of our
meeting could best be described as fraught, but I really need to take
this trip, and I need someone young and capable to come with me.
You seem like the ideal candidate to make the journey. One – you
are young. Two – your schedule can best be described as "loose".
Three – you're sitting right here. And four – I sense that you are still
feeling some residual guilt at having recently pretended to be my
dead son. You're perfect!'

James found himself smiling at Tamara Higginson's confidence
and infectious drive, and he found himself seriously considering
her proposal. And she was pretty close to accurate about his schedule. He assumed that Sophie would understand if he left with the
old woman; after all, it was kind of part of what they now did. He
loved his job at the cinema – there was no way he was going to
let himself lose it – but maybe he didn't have to. If the trip wasn't
too long he supposed he could always get Cash to fill in for him.
It was possible.

He had options.

Tamara Higginson clearly had plans.

But wasn't he the one who was supposed to have the clever
plans? Quite suddenly he'd gone from being the puppetmaster

to being the puppet. And it was one of those horrid puppets, the ones with strings. The ones that murdered people in cheap horror films. He felt like he was probably going to do whatever Tamara Higginson wanted him to do, but he didn't want to seem like a pushover. He asked her: 'So, assuming I went with you, how long would this road trip be?'

'We would be gone for a week. Ten days at the most. I would cover all of our expenses, and we would live well – otherwise, why bother? Then we would return to Melbourne and I would begin the tedious process of moving in to your loony bin,' said Tamara. 'Do we have a deal? Are you going to join me on my last great adventure, James?'

'Yes. Yes, I will, Tamara. When do we leave?'

'That depends. When is my daughter coming back for her pound of flesh?'

'Tomorrow,' said James, 'in the afternoon.'

'Excellent, then we shall leave in the morning. I say let her sweat it out for a while. It's probably character-building. Why don't you go home to pack, come back here and stay the night, and we'll leave in the morning?' Tamara offered graciously.

'Jesus,' thought James, 'this is really happening.' He desperately needed to talk it all through with someone, and when I say someone, I mean Sophie.

'That sounds great to me,' he said, trying not to show his sudden nerves to Tamara. 'But I've had about five too many vodkas to make sensible packing decisions. Let me ring Sophie, and Cash – one of them can bring over my stuff.'

'By all means,' said Tamara. 'I'd rather like to meet your friends. And in the meantime, I'll make a pot of tea.'

'Tea would be lovely,' said James.

'Is chamomile all right?' she asked.

'Chamomile is perfect.'

James called Cash to make sure that he would be home if Sophie came by to pick up his stuff, which was Tamara's suggestion. According to her, if Sophie willingly went out of her way to pick up his gear and drop it over, it meant that she liked him. A lot. James also arranged for Cash to take over cleaning his beloved cinema for the time that he would be away. Cash loved the Byron Bay plan. He was a sucker for spontaneous travel. Cash always said, 'Romance isn't sex, romance is travel. A journey speaks of possibilities yet to be revealed. Fucking is far less romantic than stepping onto a train or a 747 with someone you love.' He told James he'd be at the apartment and he'd wait for Sophie's call.

James then called Sophie. In truth he could easily have made it the couple of kilometres to his flat and picked up his stuff by himself. He wasn't that drunk. But he wanted Sophie.

He suddenly felt a need for her opinion on this whole deal. He wanted her to come over and meet Tamara, to listen to the plan, to tell him if he was a) losing his mind by agreeing to head off to Byron with a woman he'd known for a few hours, or b) doing something essential, something that simply should be done. In the brief time he'd known Tamara Higginson he had been quite taken by her. If Sophie felt the same way, then he would know he was doing the right thing.

'Soph? I need your help with something.'

'Sure,' said Sophie, a bit surprised by how vulnerable James sounded, but secretly also a bit pleased that he was calling. 'Name it.'

'Tamara wants me to go to Byron Bay with her tomorrow. She said if I do this she will leave home and move into the Peggy Day. It would only be for a few days, and she is a fantastic woman, but I need your opinion. I've told her that you're going to pick up some of my stuff from Cash and drop it off here. That way you can meet her and tell me if you think that I'm losing my mind by agreeing to do this. What do you think?'

'Oh, James, you lost your mind years ago,' said Sophie, completely intrigued now. 'I'll be over there as soon as possible.'

And with that they hung up and James went back inside, beaming.

'How did you go?' Tamara asked James.

'So far, so good,' he replied. 'My flatmate will be there for Sophie to swing by and pick up some of my stuff. Oh, shit – how late is it?'

'It's not. It's about seven-thirty. It just feels late because you and I started drinking at lunchtime, which is certainly not something that I usually do. And don't worry about the time. She's your girl-friend and you're about to disappear for a week . . .'

'She's not my girlfriend,' said James quickly.

'Well, you obviously love the woman. The only reason she's not your girlfriend is that you, James, are not a closer.'

'I'm not a what?'

'James, in this world there are people who are openers, and people who are closers. Openers are fine; they are nice people. They facilitate. They are light and fun; they bring people and situations together. But they rarely benefit directly from those situations themselves. Having brought everything to the verge of completion, they don't really know what to do next. But a closer? A closer knows what to do next.'

'And I assume that you are a closer?' said James.

'Actually, James, I am both. Opener *and* closer, alpha and omega.'

'So am I!' he insisted.

'If Sophie wants to stay, the only room that's made up is Robert's old room. The two of you can share it. Make of that what you will,' Tamara told him slyly.

'Ah!' said James. 'I think I know what you mean.'

'You know, James Rogers,' said Tamara. 'You may just be a closer after all.'

An hour later, after a quick trip to see Cash, Sophie pulled up in Tamara's driveway. (So many driveways, so little time!) The front door opened and she was confronted by the smiling faces of James Rogers and Tamara Higginson. It was immediately apparent to her that the two of them were very comfortable in each other's company. Almost like old friends.

'Hi, captain,' said James. 'Sophie Glass, meet Tamara Higginson.'

'Hello, Mrs Higginson,' said Sophie, taking the older woman's offered hand.

'Don't call her Mrs Higginson, she'll have you killed,' said James.

After a brief tour of the house, they returned to the kitchen–dining area where Tamara and James had spent most of the day. As Tamara made more tea, Sophie handed James a small backpack that was about as full as a small backpack could be.

'Okay,' she told him. 'This is going to have to do. There's a couple of pairs of jeans, a hoodie, some shirts, T-shirts, socks, underwear . . .'

'You've been in my underwear drawer?' asked James.

'Not really, no. They were all in the dryer. Cash said that you pretty much get dressed straight from the dryer.'

'I do not!' he said.

'How very sweet,' interjected Tamara.

While Tamara and Sophie sat down on the couches to get to know each other, James cooked some more rice and heated up the leftover dhal for Sophie. He looked at the two women talking and thought about how everything was moving so fast. He'd known one of these people for a couple of months and the other for less than a day, and yet he felt connected to both of them. He hoped that Sophie and Tamara would become friends, and as he watched them talking and giggling, whispering and moving closer together, he realised that he didn't have to hope very hard.

'What are you two talking about? I'm feeling left out,' he said.

'Tamara just told me you pretended to be her son today. That's pretty disgusting, James.'

'It was your idea!' he replied. 'You're the one who met with Catherine and sent me on this fool's errand . . . Anyway, Tamara pretended to be blind. That's not very cool!'

'Oh James, stop dobbing on people,' said Sophie.

He put Sophie's food down in front of her. 'Here is your dinner, you ungrateful human.'

James was loving all of this so much it was making him dizzy. He and Cash had often talked about how in life sometimes you were lucky enough to experience perfect moments, brief grabs of time when everything was heightened and beautiful and there was nowhere that you would rather be. They were rare, bright, glorious moments that balanced out the occasional darkness and made life the wonderful ride that it is. This was one of those moments and James Rogers wanted it to go on forever.

Sophie agreed to run interference with Catherine. If she were to get in touch, Sophie would tell her that she didn't know what Tamara's plans were and that Catherine would be better off speaking directly to her mother. Tamara did seem to be warming up to the idea of living at the Peggy Day Home, though. At least there she would have people to talk with, to laugh with. 'And,' she told them, 'someone has to keep an eye on the two of you.'

Sophie and James assured Tamara that living in one of the larger units at the home (which she clearly had the money for) would not be unpleasant at all. 'Seriously,' said James, 'those places are bigger than my apartment. I mean, sure, it's not this house, but you could make it your own.'

After Tamara had gone to bed, Sophie and James cleaned up and then eventually made their way upstairs, down the corridor and into the room once occupied by the person that James had earlier that day been pretending to be. The room was, like many people's old rooms in their family home, a kind of potted history of the person Robert once was. There was everything from children's drawings and model cars to a signed poster of Johnny Depp from the film *Blow* and a rudimentary but seemingly functional homemade bong. And in the middle of the room stood a downlit, king-sized four-poster bed with a canopy hanging around it that meant you could make it into a sort of room within a room, kind of bohemian and romantic, and incredibly hard to ignore. Any anxiety being felt by Sophie and James (and there was *heaps* of it) was amplified by the downlighting. The bed may as well have had neon arrows pointing at it and a flashing sign saying: 'You are both about to get in this!' Or: 'Don't forget, this can be used for other things than just sleeping!'

'Wow,' said Sophie, taking in the room. 'How are you feeling?'

'I'm . . . I'm feeling nervous. Yep, I don't think nervous is too strong a word. I also feel awkward. Like I've just moved into a flat at 39 Awkward Street, Stress Town, Anxietyville, 3182. I also feel safe while I'm talking. I feel like as long as I keep talking I won't have to deal with any of the things that I'm feel—'

Sophie put her finger to his lips. The gesture was meant to be practical but came across to both of them as intimate. It was becoming increasingly difficult to do anything that didn't seem layered.

'What do you want to do?' asked Sophie.

'What do you think?' said James.

Sophie let out an exasperated groan and leaned her head against his chest.

'Fuck!' she said.

'Exactly,' he replied.

'No, James! We can't! Not here,' said Sophie. 'I mean, you have no idea how much I want to, but not here . . .'

'Why not? We both want to. The bed obviously wants us to. And I reckon Johnny Depp would want us to.'

'I know! But I'm not fucking in Tamara's house. In her dead son's room. Do you understand what I mean?'

'Yes,' replied James, 'of course I do.'

'Good. Thank you,' she said and hugged him close.

'We could do it in the garden,' he suggested.

'Shut up, James!' She pushed away from him, laughing. 'Or I will punch you.'

He moved towards her and dragged her back into his chest, not wanting that feeling to end.

'Have you noticed,' he asked, 'how punching or the threat of punching is about as intimate as our relationship gets? What does that say about us as a couple?'

'Are we a couple?' she asked. And with that they fell into a kiss. A real kiss. A kiss that was not only their first real kiss but had the added bonus of being a great kiss for all of those involved. Some first kisses are not great. Some first kisses are hideous. Sometimes they are first and last kisses because one of the people doing the kissing has a tongue like a violent escaped prisoner who has been cornered by the police and refuses to be taken alive. But this was a kiss to build a dream on.

'I'm really glad that we did that standing up and fully clothed,' said Sophie, feeling as though she was made of liquid.

They both stood facing the bed.

'So what do we do now?' asked James.

'Well, we just get undressed and get in that, I suppose,' said Sophie. 'Can I use your toothbrush, and borrow a T-shirt to sleep in?'

'Sure,' said James, going to the backpack and finding one for her. Sophie went off in search of the bathroom to change and brush her teeth, and James hurriedly stripped down to his underwear. He folded everything neatly, placed it all on a chair and put his shoes together underneath it. He then jumped into the bed, pulled the doona down to around his waist and tried to look casual. He felt extremely formal. Then, suddenly, he thought: 'Shit. When she comes back into the room and sees me like this, she's going to think I'm naked!' He leapt out of the bed and tried standing next to it, looking relaxed. It wasn't working. He then saw his pile of clothes and decided that neatly folding them had been a mistake; it made him look anal. He crossed to the clothes and tried to mess them up a little, throwing his shirt onto the floor and kicking his shoes around a bit. He felt like he was seventeen again, a nervous but not altogether unpleasant feeling.

After a wait of what seemed to James to be about four years but was in fact more like four minutes, Sophie returned, and to James she was the personification of perfection, in a pair of simple cottontail undies and his big daggy T-shirt.

'My god,' he said. 'If I was a woman I would wear that outfit every single day.'

'You'd get cold,' she replied.

'Not if I lived in Hawaii.'

'Why are you standing next to the bed looking awkward?' she asked.

'I wanted you to see that I still have my underpants on.'

'Okay. Well, thanks, that's certainly good to know . . . Are you holding your stomach in?'

'Yes,' he replied.

'Get in bed, you idiot.'

And they did, pulling the canopy down for the full Omar Sharif, tent-in-the-desert effect. They lay on their backs for a while and talked about Tamara Higginson and Byron Bay and what was to come. After a while they both rolled onto their sides, their arms around each other. They didn't talk any more because they didn't have to, and every part of their bodies where skin met skin felt like a promise.

The next morning when they woke up together for the first time things were sickly sweet. Lots of long desiring gazes, and now that they had broken the kissing barrier, there was quite a bit of that also. Neither of them seemed to mind that they hadn't had sex. Even Johnny Depp didn't seem to mind; but, having said that, it can often be hard to tell what actors are really thinking. Especially posters of actors.

'How did you sleep?' asked Sophie as she got up.

'Brilliantly,' he said. 'How about you?'

'It was nice having you there,' said Sophie, borrowing James' toothbrush for the second time in eight hours.

'Did I snore?' asked James.

'Not at all,' lied Sophie as she slipped out the door and headed to the bathroom.

*

By the time the two of them made it downstairs Tamara had two big suitcases by the door and was busying herself with making preparations for their departure.

'Hello, young people. How did you sleep?'

'Beautifully, thank you, Tamara,' said Sophie. 'And you?'

'I was a little excited about our trip to Byron, but I did eventually doze off. There's breakfast things in the kitchen, help yourself.'

Sophie and James did just that. Alongside a pot of delicious coffee, there were ham and cheese croissants, bacon and egg rolls, fruit and pastries. James was delighted.

'Tamara, did you make all of this?' he asked.

'Oh please, be serious. I made the coffee but the rest I had delivered.'

'It's hard to fault a woman who dials out for breakfast,' said James. 'I think I'm going to like travelling with you.'

'Would you like to see the Jaguar? After all, you will be doing all the driving,' said Tamara.

James was not a car nut. Living in St Kilda meant that he didn't need one. He was close enough to everything he needed to be close to, and efficient public transport, cabs and Uber meant that he hadn't owned a car for the last couple of years. But as the three of them stood in front of the garage and Tamara used the remote to open the door, he suddenly found himself hoping it would be a great car.

It was.

'It's stunning,' said Sophie as the door opened and revealed a late-model Jaguar that was as feline as its namesake.

'I don't know much about it,' said Tamara. 'But it's reliable, comfortable and fast. And it has an amazing sound system and an engine the size of a small European country.'

'I reckon it's perfect,' said James. 'Is it insured?'

'Yes, James, it's insured. Just how badly are you intending to drive it?'

'Just making sure . . .'

At 10.47, kisses and hugs were exchanged (no handshakes required). Sophie closed Tamara's car door for her and James slipped in behind the wheel.

'I think this may be the most comfortable seat I've ever sat in,' he said.

'Good,' replied Tamara. 'You are going to be sitting in it a lot over the coming days.'

Sophie gave James a final brief kiss and a seriously meaty punch on the shoulder and then he pulled the Jag out on to what Winston Churchill had once lovingly called 'the road, baby, the motherfucking road'.

Exactly seventy-eight metres up the motherfucking road, James pulled the car over. In their excitement about their journey, neither of them had bothered to find out how you actually get to Byron Bay.

'I assumed that you would know how to get there,' said Tamara.

'Why did you assume that?'

'Because you are driving the car.'

'Our phones!' exclaimed James. 'We can ask our phones.'

He took out his phone and asked Siri how to get to Byron Bay. She redirected him to Google Maps and within a minute he and Tamara were back on the road.

'We need music, James. What is a road trip without music?' said Tamara after they'd been driving for a while. She pushed a couple of buttons on the dash and James prepared himself to be open-minded. He was ready for some Vera Lynn – style tunes, or at best some kind of 1950s doo-wop numbers. What he got was *The Velvet Underground & Nico*.

'The Velvets. I'm impressed,' said James.

'Thank you, James. That's very patronising of you.'

'Oh no. I didn't mean to sound . . . I love this song. And you are . . . senior. That's all I —'

'James, pull the car over,' Tamara said abruptly.

'What?' he asked.

'Just pull over.'

He did as he was told, pulling the Jaguar onto a dry grassy verge.

'James, we have known each other for about twenty-four hours. In that time things have been somewhat amplified. We have, for various reasons, jumped ahead quite a bit on the "getting to know each other" scale.'

'I agree,' he said.

'I don't care if you agree,' she replied. 'I want to ask you, James: do I treat you as though you are a certain age? Don't bother answering, because the answer is no. I treat you as a person. The idea of spending a week with someone who is treating me like a relic of a lost age is a thought that I find extremely tedious. We are partners and we shall treat each other as equals. Do we have a deal?'

'We have a deal,' said James, contrite.

A few minutes later, as they started to pass through what James would call 'actual countryside', he asked: 'Where are we going?'

'What do you mean? We're going to Byron Bay.'

'Yes, I know that,' said James. 'But why? Who is this mysterious person that you have to see?'

'He's a very old friend,' replied Tamara. 'In so very many ways, he is the man that I should have married. His name is Baylor Petersen and I think you'll like each other very much.'

'What does he do in Byron Bay?' asked James.

'He did a lot of things before he retired. He was a musician, he was a fisherman, he was a builder . . . I went to Byron about a year after my husband's death, to relax and to regroup. I met Baylor at a restaurant one night. We were both eating alone and the restaurant was very busy. They asked if we would mind sharing a table and so we did.'

'Fate,' said James.

'Fate or economics,' replied Tamara. 'It doesn't really matter. We ate and drank and talked. Before long we had fallen into each other. I can honestly say that those years were among the happiest times of my life.'

'He must be pretty cool. And aside from Cash Driveway, he has the best name I've ever heard,' said James.

'Oh, cool doesn't come close,' said Tamara. 'Selfless is more like it. Once when we were walking along the cliffs at Byron, we saw a little girl crying hysterically. She was pointing down at the water. When we looked down, what must have been twenty metres, we could see a little dog getting thrown around onto the rocks by crashing waves.'

James was compelled, like he was watching a movie. 'What happened?' he asked.

'Well,' said Tamara, 'if I wasn't already in love with him, what happened next would've sealed the deal. Baylor casually handed me his sunglasses and jumped off the cliff into the water. Like it was nothing. He missed the rocks by about a foot. He swam over, grabbed the dog and made it back to shore. He gave the dog to the little girl and said to me, "How about I put on some dry clothes and we go out for lunch?" I swooned.'

'What?' said James looking very impressed but also anxious. 'He sounds like a superhero! I'm going to feel pathetic when we meet.'

'Oh, relax,' said Tamara. 'He's not quite that dynamic these days.'

'So why didn't you stay together?' asked James.

'We did. For about ten years, moving between Byron and Melbourne. But we were both old and proud and stubborn. Both of us kept expecting the other one to drop their life and move. And eventually we realised that was never going to happen, so we decided to just return to our own lives and see each other when we could, when we wanted to.'

'And how did that work out?'

'Remarkably well. We both travelled back and forth; it seemed free and the best possible way to live. Now this will probably be my last trip to visit him. I wanted it to feel right, and it does.'

'I'm not cramping your style? I'm still not quite sure why you even wanted me to come.'

'Because, James, as George Mallory said about Mount Everest, you were there. You also seemed smart and kind and interesting. But more importantly, and don't take this the wrong way, please, you seem as though you're looking for something. I don't really care what it is you're looking for; the point is you're looking, and an inquiring mind is an attractive mind.'

'And I can drive,' added James.

'Yes, that was important too,' she said.

'I hope you feel safe with me,' said James.

Tamara answered in the affirmative, but not with words. Instead, about two minutes later she promptly and very gracefully fell asleep.

As they were in no particular hurry they decided to take the slightly slower but more scenic route that would see them travelling from Melbourne out down near the coast, then through the national parks to Canberra before going inland to Sydney and following the coast road all the way to Byron.

'According to Google Maps it's about three hours more than if we just gunned it straight there,' James had said.

'We're not "gunning it" anywhere. We have all the time in the world. Let's go the beautiful way,' Tamara replied.

'You mean by aeroplane?' prodded James.

'Oh James. Do you equate car trips with boredom?'

'Yes,' he said.

'That may well be because the people that you have been on car trips with in the past were boring people. I, on the other hand, am not boring, so we won't have that problem, or at least you won't. And we will be travelling through some stunning scenery. Appreciate it, for god's sake. Boredom is a lost art, as is transit. And I worry about that. These days we are never alone, not really; we're always findable, and distraction is usually just an app away. Of course boredom was never fun, but it had its uses. Some of the best inventions the world has ever seen were the direct result of boredom. If cave people or the earliest forms of man had iPhones, I don't think the wheel would ever have been invented.'

'Maybe not,' said James. 'But they would have had Menulog and Twitter. They would've been all, "Hey Grug, my car hasn't got any wheels but I've just had an excellent risotto from Chiccio's. #GoodTimes."'

'You are extremely annoying, James,' said Tamara.

'Yes,' he replied. 'But I'm funny – a bit. Aren't I?'

'A bit. But "funny" is not a quality that I particularly rate. "Funny" is best reserved for clowns and those terrible festival people that come out every April.'

They stopped for petrol and something to eat at a roadhouse in Moe, a town with a *Twin Peaks* vibe. As they pulled away eating their takeaway food, James laughed to himself.

'What?' asked Tamara.

'Oh, nothing, really,' he said. 'It's just, I have never heard anyone order a Chiko roll with such dignity: "I believe I'll have the Chiko roll with some soy sauce, please",' he said, doing a terrible, posh impression of her voice.

'Well, I'm not going to hide my education simply because I'm faced with limited culinary options. Anyway, you are eating steamed dim sims, which makes any opinion you express quite void of meaning for at least the next hour.'

Tamara had The Pretenders on the stereo. James turned it up louder as they pulled onto the highway, both of them smiling into the sun.

By the time they got to Canberra, it was late. James parked the car outside the hotel Tamara had booked, and as they got out he stretched and breathed in air that was much thinner than he was used to.

'What, no valet parking?' he asked Tamara with mock outrage.

'I'm sorry, are you terribly disappointed?'

'I was kind of looking forward to it being like a movie. You know, tossing the keys to some young guy in a suit, slipping him a twenty-dollar note and saying something cool.'

'Like what?' she asked.

'I don't know. Something like "G'day, mate. Whatcha reckon of me car?"'

'Very cool,' smiled Tamara. 'Are you hungry? Do you want to find somewhere for dinner?'

'Not really. I'm more tired than hungry.'

'Excellent. I agree. Let's just sleep and then have a ridiculously large breakfast tomorrow morning.'

'Best plan ever,' said James.

After they had checked in, James, wearing his backpack, dragged Tamara's suitcases up to her room. When he had lifted the two big bags onto the shelves provided, he stood there panting for a moment.

'Thank you, James. Tomorrow night we'll stay somewhere with valet parking and staff to carry bags,' said Tamara. 'I rather like the idea of you tossing the keys to some chap. And we have to try to spend as much of Catherine's money as possible in the next few days.'

'Your money,' he corrected her.

'You know, I don't usually surround myself with outrageous displays of wealth. It all feels very shallow. It's wonderful to have nice things, but there are limits . . . Have you ever seen the film *Chariots of Fire?*' she asked suddenly.

'Sure,' said James. 'The Paris Olympics, Eric Liddell, not running on Sunday because he was a Christian. I love that film.'

'Well, you know the section where a wealthy English athlete is practising on his estate, and he has hurdles set up for 100 metres on his beautifully manicured lawn and his butler places a half-full glass of champagne on each hurdle? The idea is that he hits the hurdles with his foot as he clears them, but not hard enough to knock the champagne off. And do you remember what the athlete says as he's about to launch himself down the line? He turns to his butler, who is standing there holding a half-full bottle of champagne, and he says something like, "Touch but don't spill, Peters. Touch but don't spill." And you know, ever since seeing the film thirty-odd years ago, that particular line of dialogue returns to me again and again. I've come to think of it as a kind of metaphor for life. Touch but don't spill . . . Goodnight, James Rogers,' she said, smiling warmly.

'Goodnight, Tamara Higginson,' said James, closing the door to her room and going to his own.

'Touch but don't spill,' he thought to himself, nodding.

Like a lot of places that were designed on a flat piece of paper, Canberra is at its most impressive when viewed from above. From the balconies of their respective hotel rooms the next morning, James and Tamara admired the nation's capital as they both made phone calls, Tamara to Catherine and James to Sophie.

Tamara told Catherine what she and James were doing. She told her about having faked most of the medical conditions and why she had felt she needed to do so. She also told her daughter that in a week or so, when she and James returned from Byron Bay, she would be moving out of the house and into the Peggy Day Home with a minimum of fuss. Catherine was relieved. When they rang off both women felt they could breathe easier, and they did. So all in all, a good phone call.

As was James and Sophie's.

'So what's it been like?' she asked. 'Where are you?'

'Canberra. We stayed here last night, about to smash a huge breakfast and then on to beautiful Byron Bay,' he said, sounding like a poorly made ad for a travel company.

'I'm so jealous. Is it like some huge adventure?'

'Yeah, It's been pretty cool. I always forget how varied the landscapes of this country are. And it's only going to get better. It's kind of like a geographical representation of getting to know you.'

'Shut up, dickhead,' she said.

'God, you are romantic,' he replied. 'How's Mrs Murphy? She'll be out waiting by her tree in exactly one hour and fifty-three minutes.'

'She will indeed. I'll send her your love.'

'I can't believe I'm not going to see you for a week,' he said.

'I know,' replied Sophie. 'But I think you're doing something really important. And when you get back and Tamara moves into the home, the three of us can hang out together all the time.'

'Great,' he said. 'And the next time we are in the same bed . . .'

'I've been imagining what it will be like,' Sophie said shyly.

'Well, don't imagine it too much. I mean, don't imagine it being too good. Imagine it being awkward and terrible so that when we actually . . .'

'Shut up, James. You are an idiot,' she laughed.

'I better go. I'll call you tonight, when we get there,' he said. 'Bye, beautiful.'

'Bye, dickhead,' she replied.

Thirty minutes later James and Tamara were sitting in the middle of the hotel's restaurant. As a barista made them coffee Tamara turned to James and asked, 'Have you ever fed toast to a horse?'

'No. No I haven't,' he replied, surprised.

'Hmm. It seems there are a lot of things you haven't done,' said Tamara philosophically.

'What is that supposed to mean?' he asked.

'Nothing,' she replied. 'It was just an observation. Now let's eat. I'm starving.'

*

After what they both agreed was an astoundingly good breakfast they got back in the car and hit the road. James was in charge of the music that day and he opened the voyage with an American mix that he'd made years before. Tamara continued to impress and annoy James with her knowledge of music – even if she didn't know the band or the song, she knew something about it, like who wrote it or who made the film clip.

'How come you know so much about music that is, dare I say it, "of another generation"?' he asked.

'Because I listen, James. It's quite a good thing to do. And it's not "of another generation". If I'm alive while something is being made, played or performed, as far as I'm concerned, it's being made, played and performed for me to enjoy. Don't limit yourself so much. Go out, do something that surprises you. Feed toast to a horse. Live in —'

'Excuse me!' broke in James. 'What is with feeding toast to horses? Is that even a thing?'

'I don't know if it's "a thing", but I have done it. It's kind of as you would imagine, really. Like feeding toast to any large animal. I just wanted to think of something that you hadn't done and see if I could make you obsess about it. Have you been obsessing about it?'

'Yes. Yes, I have. I haven't been able to concentrate properly since you first said it.'

'Then you are simply going to have to do it. Feed some toast to a horse. Conquer your demons. We'll stop at the next roadhouse, buy some toast, and have an equine picnic,' she said.

James reached over, across Tamara, and opened the glove box in front of her. Inside, very neatly displayed, resting on one of the red serviettes from the hotel restaurant, were two pieces of wholemeal toast.

'I'm way ahead of you,' he said, ridiculously proud of himself.

Soon they were standing against a wire fence on a side road off the highway, feeding toast to a couple of very grateful horses.

'This is pretty rad,' said James. 'It's kind of exciting because they almost bite your fingers off.'

'Everyone knows that horses like carrots and apples, but only a select group of people, of whom you are now one, also know the giddy delight that a horse gets from eating a simple piece of toast.'

'They sure do,' he said. 'If I'd known how much they were going to enjoy it, I would've buttered it back at the hotel.'

'Oh, don't be ridiculous, James. You can't feed butter to a horse!'

Back in the car, as he was about to turn the key and fire up the Jaguar, James stopped and surprised himself by turning to Tamara and asking, 'What do you think happened to your son? To Robert?'

Tamara paused for a moment, adjusted herself in the seat and looked into James' face.

'To be honest, I can't answer that question definitively,' she said.

'I'm sorry, we don't have to talk about it . . .'

'Oh no,' said Tamara, 'it's fine. In fact, I'd rather like to talk about him. It's just that so much of what happened at the end is a mystery. More questions than answers. And when you're a parent, no matter what the evidence says, you always hold out a terrible kind of hope that one day your child will walk back through the door, even if you know that's not possible. Even if you know that your child is dead.'

'Are you sure this is okay to talk about?' asked James nervously. 'I don't want to upset you.'

'It's fine, James. In fact, it's good. I've actively not talked about him for a very long time and I now think that was a mistake. My beautiful, silly, crazy Robert . . . Are you sure that *you're* ready for this?' she asked him.

'Of course. I'd be honoured,' he said. And as he started the car and pulled out onto the road in the beautiful morning light, Tamara Higginson told James Rogers about the loss of her son.

'He was a very kind and loving child, but Robert was an escalator,' she said, 'in that from an early age he would escalate any situation that he found himself in. If something was bad he would make it worse; if something was dangerous he would make it life-threatening. But, on the flip side, if something was good he would make it perfect. He was a very bright boy but he realised very early on that he didn't have to work hard to succeed. By the time he was fourteen he had become part of a group of boys who pre-ferred smoking and skulking around the city to actually attending school and studying. In fact for an institution that cost around ten thousand dollars a year in fees, with alumni including prime min-isters and captains of industry, his school produced a remarkably high number of fairly infamous criminals. Mostly white-collar, going to prison for financial crimes or having assets stripped by the tax department.'

'Sounds like they may have known my father,' interjected James.

'Really, why is that?'

'No, no, keep going,' said James.

'Robert, unlike some of his friends, actually finished school with good enough marks to get him into Melbourne University, but instead he drifted towards criminality. He and his friends embarked upon numerous failed careers, growing dope crops on the coast or trying to deal drugs to the nightclub crowd. He was never a violent person but I think he liked to surround himself with the unpredictable possibilities of that world. Sadly, and in a strange way understandably, I think he found the real world, our world, uncomfortable. Like a suit that simply did not fit him . . . Am I boring you yet?' she asked.

'Anything but,' said James. 'You'll know when I'm bored because the car will leave the road and crash into a tree.'

'Oh, well that's nice to know,' said Tamara before continuing. 'Like everyone in our family, Robert loved to travel, and most of the time I don't think he cared where he travelled to. He just enjoyed being out of his comfort zone, assuming he ever even had a comfort zone. At one point, through a very old friend of mine in the music industry, I got him a job in New York. He was assistant manager at a rock venue in the Bowery, but he didn't stay there for very long. In hindsight it may have been a mistake to send someone with a fascination for the drug trade to work in New York's East Village surrounded by punk rockers and drag queens.

'After that he came back to Australia and for the next few years he would travel to another country, stay for a little while, and then return home. The fact that many of these trips were to Asian or South American countries would probably have been a red flag to most mothers in my situation but by then I was quite defeated by it all.' She paused for a moment, remembering difficult things, before shaking herself slightly and continuing.

'The last time I saw my son he was heading off to England to spend time with old friends. I recall that he seemed happier than I had seen him in years . . . And then he simply vanished. The police told us that after he'd been in London for a few days he had with-drawn twenty thousand pounds from his bank account. At first I hoped that he was simply on another nefarious adventure, but a week later Scotland Yard called to tell us that they had found his briefcase and his passport abandoned in the dirt on the side of the M1. He would never have left those things behind willingly. The briefcase had been a gift from his father, and he loved it very much. And any kind of journey that he was going on without his passport was only ever going to be a short and brutal one. It pains me to think of how frightened he must've been at the end . . . He would have been terrified, don't you think?'

'I hope not,' replied James, feeling honoured to be hearing this but also as though he was eavesdropping on something deeply personal.

'Orphan; widow; widower,' said Tamara. 'There are names for those who have lost the people they love. We give them names because we feel for them. But there is no name for those who've lost children. Not in our language. That is a bridge too far.'

They drove for a long time without talking. James shifting the Jag into fifth gear was the only hint at just how fast his heart was racing. He took a deep breath.

'I'm so very sorry about your son,' he said.

Tamara briefly placed her hand over his on the gearstick and then turned to look at James, side on, as he drove. She knew he could see her looking but deliberatelely said nothing. She was pushing him, because she could. Eventually he shot her a glance and said, 'What? What are staring at me for?'

She held his gaze and said, 'James, I admire the fact that you ask questions, that you are interested in other people, but I've noticed something about you – you ask but you don't tell.'

'What do mean?' asked james, knowing exactly what she meant.

'You talk about Sophie and Cash, but that's about it. Don't you know anyone else?'

'I know a Thai guy called Graham.'

'What about your parents? What did they do?'

James made an 'ouchy' face before replying, 'Well, my mother was a mother and fairly recently she died in the place that you are about to move into. So that's a cheerful topic.'

This didn't throw Tamara at all. She carried on as though they were discussing the weather. 'That's what old people do, James – we die. You mentioned your father earlier. Tell me about him.' She had a way of making James do things, even if he didn't want to do them.

'He died too, but . . .'

James stopped talking. He looked deeply uncomfortable, a look Tamara had not seen on his face before.

'But what? Come on, James. It's your turn to share something personal.'

James pulled the car over to the side of the road and turned to face Tamara. 'Are you sure you want to hear this?'

'Oh, James, are you serious? Can you imagine anyone, and I mean *anyone*, saying no to that question? Of course I want to hear it. I mean, it must be intense; you stopped driving, for god's sake.'

He leaned back in the driver's seat and exhaled deeply.

'Okay,' said James, 'here we go. My father was an investment banker. A big one. His name was Bill Rogers . . .'

Tamara cut him off. 'You don't mean "Dollar Bill" Rogers? He was your father?' She looked shocked.

'Do want to hear the story?' said James grumpily. 'I mean, fuck, this isn't exactly my favourite thing to talk about. He mucked up a lot of people's lives. Including mine . . .' James paused, looking slightly lost. 'So you know who he was?'

Tamara raised an eyebrow. 'James, I think everybody knows who he was. I'm not trying to be rude, but . . . He was Dollar Bill Rogers. I mean, he was famous. Up there with Skase and Alan Bond. Although I'm not sure I ever heard the full story?'

James looked straight ahead and started the story.

'My father, who was essentially a good man, pulled off the largest ponzi scheme in Australian history. He was a financial genius who made millions of dollars for thousands of people. But he was so confident, and so used to being right, that when the crash came and the market went to shit, he just couldn't see it or accept it. He honestly believed that he could ride it out – turn it around. You see, he'd never been wrong. Never. And that is a dangerous thing. So he started taking risks, big risks, with other people's money. He was 100 per cent convinced that he would win, that he would triumph, and everyone would keep getting rich. And then it got worse. So, like a gambling addict, he doubled down. Again. And again. Eventually, he couldn't stop; he was in too deep. It was all falling apart. He ruined the lives of his friends, his family. A couple of people lost everything; at least one committed suicide. Because of my dad. A man so blinded by success that he simply couldn't comprehend failure. When the police came for him, I was the one who opened the door for them. I remember being deeply impressed by their uniforms. I was nine.'

James exhaled and drummed on the steering wheel.

'When they took him away, I didn't realise he was going to end up in jail. I didn't go to the court case – that day was the last time

I ever saw him. The most confident, able man I have ever met was reduced to a confused mess. As a kid, it is terrifying to see your invincible father broken like a stick. They walked him out the door and he looked like the victim of a terrible misunderstanding, or like someone who had lost his keys. The last thing he said to me was, "I'm so sorry, Jimmy. I've just got to go sort some things out." And I think he honestly believed he could. Just sort it out. Three days later, he died of a heart attack in prison. Dollar Bill Rogers. A man who had been right too many times to understand that he was deeply, deeply wrong.

'My mother was both heartbroken and humiliated in equal measure. Most of my parents' so-called friends dropped her immediately. It was just too awkward to have her around. Claudia and I became her life. To make sure that we could eat and finish school, she had to work for the first time in her life. For two years she worked in the local fish and chip shop, where every Friday her former friends would drop in and buy their dinner. I know she felt ashamed at our sudden fall, but she also felt pride. She would do anything for her children. If it meant working in a fish shop, so be it.'

Tamara reached over and placed her hand on his cheek. 'Oh, James. I'm so sorry.'

James smiled awkwardly, and then suddenly he was serious again. 'You know, I wish we'd never had money. Being rich, and then suddenly being kind of poor? It sucks. It's like being given a birthday cake or a pony called Tarquin, and then having someone take it away, saying, "Oh, sorry, there's been a mistake; this is for someone else."'

He smiled again. 'I resent every rich person on earth – except you.'

They got to Coffs Harbour just in time to watch the sun go down behind the Big Banana, a vast walk-through reproduction of a piece of fruit.

'Why?' asked Tamara, echoing a question that must've been asked by hundreds of thousands of people over the years.

'I'm not sure,' said James. 'Maybe it's here to dissuade alien invaders? Maybe if they see this they'll think, "Shit, if their bananas are this big, their people must be huge. Let's leave."'

'I don't think aliens would fall for that. I mean, it's got "The Big Banana" painted on the outside,' replied Tamara.

While Tamara and James were philosophising over the relative merits of 'big' things, a thousand kilometres away Sophie Glass was finishing up at the Peggy Day Home. It had been a trying day and she wished that James was there with her. Just because.

Sophie's day had centred on Mrs Murphy, the woman who waited each day for her by now middle-aged twins to come visit her. Mrs Murphy had an unflinching but heartbreaking optimism. She never complained that she had been waiting that long, but rather approached each day as though it was going to be *the* day. The perfect day. The day that her children finally came to see her. So that she could tell them everything – so that she could tell them how much she had loved them.

For the entire time that she had worked at the home, Sophie had watched Mrs Murphy and her inspiring but devastating daily dance with the ghosts of possibility. While Mrs Murphy's lonely vigil had often moved Sophie to tears, she had never thought it was her place to tell the old woman to stop, to give up and accept the reality that, after twenty-eight years, her children were never going to come. But that day, as Sophie stood in her office drinking a cup of chamomile tea and gazing out at the proud old woman standing by her proud old tree, something shifted in her. She began to think about the wasted hours that Mrs Murphy had spent in her quest for . . . what? Redemption? Absolution? Sophie went to her desk, picked up her phone and opened the calculator app. Two hours per day × 365 days equalled 730 hours a year. And 730 hours a year × 28 years equalled 20 440 hours. Mrs Murphy had spent 851.67 days out there waiting and waiting and waiting.

'No,' said Sophie to herself fiercely. 'It's not fair.'

The twins were never coming, thought Sophie, and it was time for someone to tell her. To show her that it was all right to let go.

But *was* it all right? What if not letting go was what Mrs Murphy lived for? What if those two potent hours, those 120 minutes of anticipation, were what made the other twenty-two hours of her day bearable? Sophie had spent her life believing that you should let people do whatever they chose to do; that no person had the right to tell someone else what they could or could not do, if they weren't hurting anyone. But as Mrs Murphy's carer Sophie also felt that it was her responsibility to do what she could to improve the quality of whatever was left of her life. This was Sophie's dilemma – Sophie's choice, if you will . . .

That afternoon, Sophie went to see Mrs Murphy in her room. The old woman was reading as Sophie stood in the doorway and knocked on the open door.

'Oh hello, Sophie, don't you look beautiful,' said Mrs Murphy. 'What a nice surprise. Come in, come in. And please, sit down, you're on your feet all day.'

'Thanks, I don't mind if I do,' said Sophie, sitting down in a deep green armchair opposite her. 'How was your day?'

'Quite lovely,' replied Mrs Murphy. 'I had a wonderfully long talk with Dr Harvey this morning. Good god, that man is irascible, but also very charming.'

'Ah Dr Harvey, yes, he is quite a handful,' said Sophie, surprising herself by using a sentence that sounded like it came from the 1940s.

'He's a dark horse that one. He comes across as such a stick in the mud, but he surprised me today when he said that he was a big supporter of gay rights. He even voted Yes for marriage equality!'

'He did what?' said Sophie, genuinely shocked.

'Yes. I was extremely pleased. It seems he has a gay son of whom he is very, very proud.'

'Does he just?' said Sophie. She was stunned by Dr Harvey's turnaround, and fought the urge to get up and do a little victory dance for herself and James.

'Yes and his son came to visit him recently. It sounded quite lovely.'

With those few words Sophie became uncomfortably aware of why she was there in Mrs Murphy's room and what she had come to talk about.

'I saw you out by the oak tree earlier,' said Sophie.

'Today and every day,' smiled Mrs Murphy. 'For longer than I care to remember.'

'How was it?' asked Sophie.

'It was lovely. It always is,' replied Mrs Murphy. 'There are magpies in the tree with a four-week-old baby. It's started to fly and it's very sweet. And the adult birds never swoop me because they are used to me now and they know that I am not a threat. I have named the baby Matilda.'

'How long have you been going out to the tree now?'

'Twenty-eight years,' said Mrs Murphy without having to think about it.

'Do you think . . .' said Sophie, 'that maybe . . . it's time . . .'

'That maybe it's time I stopped?' asked Mrs Murphy.

'Yes. I just think . . . What if they aren't coming? I see you out there every day, and I worry for you.'

'Oh, Sophie, that's very kind of you,' she said. 'And you know, perhaps they won't come – but perhaps they will. And really, at my age, what is life but waiting? Waiting for dinner. Waiting for your children. Waiting for yourself. Waiting for beginnings, or for an end.'

Sophie eyes began to fill with tears. 'I just – I don't want you to feel alone.'

With that the dam burst and Sophie cried. She cried for all the hurting. She cried for Mrs Murphy, and she cried for everyone.

Her friends, her family, for the lost and the broken. She cried for Charlotte Durham and Dr Harvey. She cried for herself and for James and Tamara, somewhere on the road. She cried for old Cash Driveway. She didn't try to stop; she just cried.

'I'm sorry, this isn't very professional of me.' But the crying eased something in her and the tears kept running like rivers.

'It's okay, Sophie,' said the old woman, handing her a tissue, and then the entire box of tissues. 'You cry, my girl; it's a balm for the soul. But you needn't cry for me. I've done enough of that for a few lifetimes.'

Mrs Murphy went quiet for a minute, contemplating, and then said, 'I want to tell you something. I know that they probably won't come. My children. They have their own lives now and perhaps their own children. I am like a story to them, if that. But it doesn't really matter any more because when I'm out there, waiting, it's as though they have already arrived. They're out there in the tree, in the grass, in the sky. Even if they don't know how much I have loved them, *I* do. I know. And sometimes that's enough.'

'You are going to make me cry again,' said Sophie. After a moment, she continued, 'Mrs Murphy, do you think – would it be okay if sometimes I came and waited with you?'

'I think that would be splendid.'

I know. I know. I know.

At around nine o'clock James and Tamara drove into Byron Bay. The moon was shining on the ocean, silhouetting the mountains like in a movie, or a really describey book. James eased the Jaguar into a parking bay outside a very swanky hotel. What hotel? I'm not saying. Not until I reach a level of fame where I get sweet payola and free accommodation for name-checking such an establishment. Suffice to say, it was one of those places where everything has been thought out in advance – a place where, just as you realise you want something, it magically appears in front of you.

After Tamara had checked them in and a porter had taken their bags up to their rooms, they exchanged looks in the foyer and, without saying a word, made their way to the bar out on the verandah. It was dark and cool and James found their seats even more comfortable than his seat in the Jag. The waiter came over to their table and they ordered two extremely dry martinis.

'It feels good here,' said James as the waiter arrived with their drinks. 'And it's about to feel even better.'

'Here's to you and Sophie,' said Tamara.

'Here's to you and Baylor,' replied James.

They could hear the waves breaking as they took their first sips.

One hour and four martinis later, as they sat staring out towards the sea, Tamara asked, 'Why did you agree to this? To coming here with me?'

'I don't really know,' replied James.

'My daughter offered you ten thousand dollars. I don't imagine that is still on the table.'

'No. Probably not.'

'So why did you come?'

'I guess because we get on well,' he replied. 'And maybe I just needed to feed some toast to a horse.'

'Hmm. Perhaps,' said Tamara. 'Speaking of food and horses, how's eight o'clock for you for breakfast tomorrow?'

'Well, I have a few business meetings but I'm sure they can be rescheduled,' James replied. 'Eight sounds fine.'

Tamara nodded in approval and paid the bill, leaving a very large tip.

'You really are trying to spend all of your money, aren't you?' asked James as they made their way to the lifts.

'Oh, I've been trying for years. If you decide that you want any food and drinks or anything, just charge it back to your room.'

When he got to his room James wandered around, exploring its majesty. Unlike a lot of people, he loved hotels, especially hotels as fancy as this. He went straight to the minibar and fixed himself a vodka and ice.

Taking his drink out to the balcony James sat and pondered his good fortune. He was very aware that, of all the great things being afforded him on this trip, the greatest luxury was Tamara Higginson's companionship. He thought about this as he listened to the waves crash onto the shore. He hadn't seen the waves yet but was confident that they existed somewhere out there in the cool dark. Then, feeling like hearing from home, he called Cash Driveway.

'Hey, CD, what's up?'

'Not much, friend. I've just done a huge painting of Kim Jong-un doing a horsey off a high-diving board. It's not very subtle but at least I haven't set anything on fire. And I had lunch with Sophie today. She is a real winner – I don't know what she sees in you.'

'Thanks, friend.'

'She told me about Mrs Murphy waiting by the tree. That's a grim story – it's gothic.'

'I know. It's messed up. And she is a really nice lady. But what can you do?'

The brief shared silence translated to 'not much'.

'So I assume you guys made it to Byron. How goes it?' asked Cash.

'It's great, Cash. I'd almost forgotten how beautiful it is up here. I feel . . . lighter. How's the cinema going? How's having an actual job? I told you it was easy.'

'It sure is. I get why you love that place so much now. I actually really dig being in there when it's empty. You can really sense the history. All those movies, all those people . . .'

'And all those choc-top wrappers that you have to clean up,' said James.

'Yeah, but it is pretty cool – for a job. And speaking of "pretty cool for a job", how's Tamara? When are you guys coming back?'

'In a few days, I guess. I'll let you know.'

'Great,' said Cash, and then began a routine the two of them had shared many times. 'Now, what is the past?' he asked.

'Something that once happened,' replied James.

'What is the future?'

'Something that will be.'

'And what is the present?'

'The present is all. The present is now. The present is eternal.'

'Amen to that, brother,' said Cash before hanging up.

James Rogers and Cash Driveway shared a belief that the meaning of life was to be found in its moments, and that anyone who spent their existence romanticising the past or imagining a magical future was missing the point and was probably going to end up disillusioned.

After he had hung up, Cash went back to his painting of the North Korean leader but he couldn't concentrate. His thoughts were on his friends, and on Mrs Murphy, a woman he had never met. A woman lost in time.

He sat down at his computer and composed the following email:

To: srglass@hotmail.com
From: cashdriveway@gmail.com

Sophie.

Cash here. This is our first email! Remember today's date and we can celebrate this momentous occasion every year!

I've been thinking about Mrs Murphy and I'd like you to send me whatever information you have on her. After what you told me today, I also spoke to James, and the way that the two of you talk about her . . . It made me want to do something, or to at least try.

I know a guy who's a private investigator (don't ask) and I was thinking that maybe he could try to find her children. I mean, that's what private eyes do, isn't it? She had twins, right? A boy and a girl? That should make them easier to find, I reckon. My friend the detective is called Ken Rosalind. I'm telling you that just in case after you send me the information he wants to get in touch with you directly, and decides that I should be killed. Unlikely but possible. I don't know if he's a good private investigator or a shit one, but I know he owns handcuffs and a gun so at least he's a reasonably serious one.

Soph, I doubt very much that he'll be able to find Mrs Murphy's children but I thought I at least better have a crack at doing something about it. And like the man said, the only way for evil to triumph is for good painters to do nothing.

This is my way of trying to do something.

Yours with love,

Cash xxx

See? I told you Cash was a good unit.

*

The next morning as they sat down to breakfast James noticed that Tamara looked more frail than usual, slightly jumpy and distracted.

'You all right, champ?' he asked, watching carefully as she swallowed some heavy-duty painkillers.

'Don't try "champing" me, James; it doesn't sit well with you,' she said, and then added, 'Have you ever had spinal cancer?'

'Ah, no,' said James. 'No, I can't say that I have.'

'Well, as it happens, I do. And believe me, it is far from pleasant,' Tamara told him.

James opened his mouth but initially he couldn't speak.

'What?' he said. 'Are you serious? You have spinal cancer? This . . . this isnt part of your "thing" is it? Like pretending to be blind?' He could tell just looking at her it wasn't, though.

James stood up in a panic. 'Jesus, are you okay?'

Tamara smiled. 'Well, not really. I have spinal cancer.'

James got up and knelt next to her, and started very gently rubbing her back. They looked into each other's faces for a long time, and then he broke the silence. 'Me rubbing it isn't really helping, is it?'

'Not really,' replied Tamara. 'But I appreciate the intent.'

Returning to his seat, James looked destroyed by the news.

'Oh god,' said Tamara archly, 'don't get morbid.'

'Well, it's a pretty heavy piece of information! What's it . . . what's it like?' James asked clumsily.

'I'll make a deal with you,' she said. 'I'll tell you what it's like – *exactly* what it's like – if you promise to make me laugh.'

James thought about it for a second and then agreed. What choice did he have?

'Okay, you tell me about it and I'll make you laugh. But not if laughing is going to make your spine fall out . . .'

She gave him a 'nice try' look. He gave her an 'I wasn't trying' look. Then he took a deep breath and, with a genuinely worried look on his face, asked, 'Okay. What's it like?'

'Well, think of the worst pain – physical, emotional, spiritual, whatever – that you have ever experienced. Can you recall it?'

'Yes, but I don't think it is suitable breakfast conversation.'

'All right,' said Tamara, ignoring his comment. 'Now imagine that pain being doubled and then doubled again. Have you got that?'

'Yes,' said James. 'But this really is a shit way to start the day. And I'm not sure how funny I can be about this.'

'But these pills, the blue ones, are Endone. They take that kind of pain and wipe it out. They make the worst pain like nothing. So I can bear it.'

James thought about that and said the first thing that came into his head. 'Fuck, that's impressive. Can I have one?'

Tamara locked eyes with him. 'Are you in constant, blinding pain?'

'Well, I banged my shin on the bed this morning. *Really* hard. Does that count?'

She had him on the ropes and they both knew it. 'No, James, that doesn't count.'

'So no Endone for me?'

'No, James, no Endone for you. But you can have some more watermelon, and get me another coffee.'

'God, you are mean,' he said petulantly, rising to do as she'd said.

'I know,' said Tamara, smiling so much that James had to smile too. 'It's all part of my mysterious charm.'

James realised that nothing he said was going to make her laugh so he went to plan B. He collapsed. He lay on the floor as though he was dead. People in the restaurant looked over at him, panicked. Then James opened one eye and glanced at Tamara. A smile slowly spread across her face before bubbling into laughter.

'*Yes!*' cried James from the floor.

Tamara was applauding gently. James stood and bowed.

'It was a bit cheap,' said Tamara, 'but yes, you made me laugh.'

They were smiling at each other, but under James' smile was the pulsing feeling that something terrible was going to happen.

And, of course, it was.

After an elaborate breakfast, James and Tamara were ready to go see Baylor Petersen. On their way out to the car James said, 'Eighty-one. There were eighty-one.'

'Are you been deliberately obscure, James? Eighty-one what?'

'Eighty-one different things to eat for breakfast on that buffet.'

'You counted them?'

'Yes. Eighty-one, and that's not including drinks.'

'Don't you think that's rather obsessive?' asked Tamara.

'No, I don't. I think it's observant.'

'It's obsessive,' she replied.

'You say potato, I say observant,' said James as he opened Tamara's door for her.

As he got in behind the wheel James realised for the first time how beautiful her outfit was. Tamara was obviously making an effort for Baylor. This lent a certain vulnerability to her and made an already fascinating woman even more so.

'I just noticed how fantastic you look,' he said.

'Thank you, James. That's very observant of you. Perhaps you would have noticed earlier if you hadn't been counting every available food option in the restaurant.'

'Are you nervous?' he asked.

'About seeing Baylor? Absolutely not. I don't think I ever have been. And you don't have to be nervous about being around him either. You'll see what I mean when we get there.'

'Where is there?' said James as he switched his phone over to Google Maps.

'He is in Bangalow, the next town over. I know the way; I'll give you directions. Use your phone for something useful, like music.'

'Should we stop and get something? Like wine or whatever? What does he drink?'

'He was drinking cask white wine when we started seeing each other. And I never tried to talk him out of it and he never changed.'

'All right,' said James as he pulled the car up on the main street near the bottle shop. 'Cask white it is. I'll just be a second.'

As he got out of the car Tamara called to him: 'Be sensible. I mean there's cask white wine and there's *cask white wine*.' She was smiling. 'I know this is an oxymoron but just get the best wine you can that comes in a cardboard box.'

'I thought it decorous to get a two-litre cask,' James said, getting back behind the wheel. When the best thing you can say about a wine is that it comes in a big container, it's probably not going to be winning many awards . . .'

'Other than the award for most wine,' suggested Tamara. 'In any case, two litres is plenty. Baylor doesn't drink like he used to.'

After driving out of the township for a few minutes, they pulled off the freeway onto a side road that soon turned into a dead end. There a few cool, individual houses were grouped together, facing out over a beautiful hillside and what was clearly a very old church and cemetery.

'Wow, when was this built?' asked James as they got out of the car and began strolling towards the cemetery.

'I'm not sure exactly,' replied Tamara, 'but at least a hundred years ago. Have a look at the headstones – some of them are from World War I. I know it's a cliché but years ago, before Baylor built his house out here, he and I used to have picnics in the cemetery. It was terribly romantic.' She paused for a moment, shutting her eyes and remembering. Then quite suddenly she added, 'As well as being very beautiful, the cemetery is also segregated.'

'It's what?'

'It's segregated. Look, see the signs? There's the Catholic section, the Protestant section. Over there is the Jewish section. There is even a mysteriously named European section. That's Baylor's favourite bit: Catholic, Jewish, Protestant, and the little-known religion – European,' said Tamara. 'And this is my favourite bit.' She started walking towards a dozen or so graves without a 'grouping'. 'According to Baylor this is the "heathen section". He and I have both got a plot and, when the time comes, we will be buried here together, with the rest of the heathens.'

'Which one is Baylor's house?' asked James, looking over at the group of six homes across from the cemetery.

'The green one,' she said. 'We designed it together.'

'It looks great. Let's go meet him! God, I'm quite nervous. I'm about to meet my pretend mum's cool guitar-playing, dog-rescuing boyfriend. What if he doesn't like me? Oh god, you haven't told him about me pretending to be your son, have you?'

'No. Not yet. I've told him virtually nothing about you. I haven't really had time,' she replied.

'Great, that means he doesn't hate me yet,' said James, visibly relieved. 'That would have been an extremely shit way to meet: "Baylor Petersen, the love of my life, meet James Rogers. You remember, I told you about James – in the week I've known him he has brought me enormous pain by pretending to be my long-dead son, and further discomfort by trying to emotionally blackmail me into leaving my family home and moving into a retirement village . . ."'

'When you put it like that,' said Tamara, 'you do sound like a bit of a prick. Fortunately you are a good driver and a better cook.'

'Let's just go up and meet him,' said James. 'This feels like it could spin out of control at any stage.'

'Yes, of course,' said Tamara. 'But let's have a wine first. Open that awful cask!'

'Shouldn't we at least call Baylor and invite him to join us?'

'That is sweet of you, but he will be lying down. Every day between eleven and twelve-fifteen he has a nap. Bring the cask, James. Live a little – god knows no one else here can,' Tamara said, carefully lowering herself down on a grave and taking two wine glasses out of her bag.

'Is that cool? Sitting on the graves. I mean, I don't object, obviously, I just don't want you to get in trouble or anything,' said James, opening the cask and bringing it over to her.

'This is my plot. Baylor's and mine. We bought it seven years ago,' she said, handing James a glass to fill. 'I'll be moving in here one day, so I may as well get a feel for the place.' James was struck by the ease and seeming delight Tamara felt sitting atop her own grave.

Then she produced a third wineglass and handed it to James.

'I've already got a glass,' he said, puzzled.

'I know,' she replied, smiling. 'As do I.'

'Who's the third glass for, then?' he asked, filling it and handing it back to her.

'Absent friends,' she said lovingly, before upending the glass over the grave next to her.

'Go easy,' said James, startled.

And then he saw it.

Tamara had been leaning with her back against one of the tombstones of the double plot. Now, as she stood and raised her glass in a toast, James could see the engraving on it. It read:

BAYLOR PETERSEN
1945–2015
Fisherman. Lover. Idiot.

It took a couple of seconds for what James was seeing to sink in.

'. . . Baylor is dead?'

'I know he is, James. Come here,' she said, standing up and taking his hand in hers. They stood together like that for quite a while,

silently staring at the grave of a man who, up until about twenty seconds ago, James had been very much looking forward to meeting.

'James Rogers, this is Baylor Petersen. Baylor, this is James.
I wish you both could have met under better circumstances.'

'Oh, I don't know,' said James. 'What better circumstances are
there than sharing a two-litre cask of room-temperature white with
a dead person in a racist cemetery? Surely this is how most great
friendships are born.'

'I'm sorry I didn't tell you, James.'

'Oh, really? Well, Tamara, so am I. But the question remains –
why? Why didn't you tell me? You told me everything else about him.
Letting me know that he had died wouldn't have changed that much.'

'I know. I know that, and you know that, *now*. But you didn't
know it then. When we were planning this. If a couple of days ago
I had said, "I am perfectly happy to leave my house and move
into the Peggy Day Home for what remains of my life, but on one
condition. I have one demand that must be met before I agree to
anything. And that demand is that someone I don't know must drive
me from Armadale to Bangalow where I will pour a glass of cask
wine over the grave of a man I loved." If I'd said that, the general
consensus would've been that I was quite mad and that any requests
I had were not to be taken seriously.' The look on her face was not
one of bitterness, but more sorrow. Sadness and regret at the lack of
humanity that humans continually felt the need to display.

James reached out, put his arm around her shoulders and said,
'I wish I'd met him. I'm so very sorry for your loss. He sounds like
a wonderful man.'

'He was, James, and I'm sure the two of you would have got
on very well indeed,' she said, pulling him in closer as they stood

over the grave. 'It's still hard to accept that he is gone. He had such boundless energy and ideas. He was always inspired, every day, in every way. In the studio, on the street, reading the paper over coffee, making dinner, making love.'

'Yeah, I'm sure that you had great sex. You don't have to go into the details,' said James.

She clinked her glass against the headstone. 'He wasn't always this docile, you know.'

'Ugh! Stop it!'

Smiling at each other, they both raised a glass to the great man and drank.

'You know, if it makes you feel any better, you are the only person from Melbourne that I've told about Baylor's death,' Tamara informed James.

'Really?' he asked. 'Why?'

'Well, only Catherine had ever met him. And I just didn't tell her when he died. To be honest, she was never really taken with him anyway . . .'

'Well, I wouldn't worry about that,' said James. 'We've already established that your daughter is more taken with herself than she is with anyone else.'

Tamara laughed. 'In any case, you're the first to hear it from me. I hope you feel flattered.'

'I do,' said James, and then, 'Let's go out tonight and celebrate his life. Your life, together. There will be eating and drinking . . .'

'And dancing on the beach?' asked Tamara.

'Fuck yes, there will be dancing on the beach!' said James, proving that he must be a decent human as there were very few things he enjoyed less than dancing on beaches.

'That, James, sounds like a splendid idea,' she said.

As they got ready to leave, Tamara left the wine cask in the shadow of Baylor's headstone with two glasses.

'Baylor's next guest will join him in a glass,' said Tamara. She assured James that, even nineteen months after his death, every day Baylor received plenty of visitors who would come for a drink and a chat with their old friend. James didn't doubt it for a second.

'Maybe I should have gone for the four-litre cask after all?' he said.

'Ah yes,' replied Tamara philosophically. '"The Big Wine Cask". The most Australian of all the "big" things.'

At around this time, Cash's private investigator friend Ken Rosalind had got in touch with a 46-year-old man called Laurence Murphy and told him a story about an old lady and a tree. Three hours later Laurence Murphy was going through some papers in the attic of the house he had grown up in.

'Where is it exactly?' he had demanded of his father.

'It's up there in one of the boxes,' his father replied. 'But leave it there. It's only going to upset you.'

'You should have told us, Dad. We both love you, but you should have told us,' Laurence said before heading up the narrow stairs.

After looking through his family's junk for an hour and a half, he finally found what he had been searching for. An old hand-written letter with two names on it, one of them his. It was from someone claiming to be his mother. A woman he hadn't seen or heard from since he was a baby. Laurence read the letter and then carefully folded it up and put it in his inside jacket pocket. He stood silently in his father's attic, among the boxes, old toys and detritus of his childhood. He breathed in deeply and then exhaled slowly three times before he took out his phone and called his twin sister.

That night Tamara and James bought takeaway from a little Thai place and took it and a bottle of wine (that's right, a *bottle*) down to the beach for the celebration of Baylor Petersen and all things good. Most people had packed up for the day and they had the beach pretty much to themselves. They laid out a blanket and took in the majesty of the ocean.

After they ate they went for a walk out along the beach and on to the rocks where waves broke all around them. Eventually they wandered back to the blanket where James hooked up a small speaker to Tamara's phone and suddenly the sound of The Doors mixed with the waves. Tamara held her hand out to James. 'Come on,' she said. 'It's time to dance.'

James did as he was told and very soon the two of them were slow dancing on the sand, like a scene from a movie. James had thought that he would feel awkward or self-conscious but he didn't. Something about the combination of Tamara's surety and a day of wine that varied radically in quality made him relax.

'How did Baylor die?' asked James.

'He just went to bed and didn't wake up.'

'I guess that's good?'

'It's not ideal – dying rarely is. But if you have to die, and we all do, yes, it wasn't too bad.'

'What does that feel like?'

'What? Knowing that I will die soon? It's not terrifying, if that's what you mean. It just feels kind of inevitable. And who knows, maybe we all meet up again.'

'Do you believe that? That there is something else after this?'

'I don't know. In some ways I don't really care. If I get to hang out with Baylor and my son and everyone else I ever knew, that would be great. If there is simply nothing after this, I won't care because I won't know.'

'Yeah,' said James, 'I guess you're right. You know, I'm so glad to have done this. This trip, to get to know you. And when you're at the Peggy Day, I'll come to see you all the time.'

'I'm sure you will. I'm a very charming woman.'

'That you are,' said James as he stopped dancing. 'I have to go sit down. I'm not used to cask wine combined with surprise deaths and dancing on beaches.'

As James sat, he watched Tamara. She was dancing with Baylor Petersen, and it was beautiful. A few minutes later his phone rang.

'Is that Sophie?' called Tamara.

'Hi, Tamara,' shouted Sophie.

Tamara walked over and took the phone from James, before walking away back down towards the water.

'Where are you two going?' he asked.

'That's none of your business. It's time for some girl talk. Relax, we'll be back in a few minutes.'

Tamara wandered off down along the beach, chatting into the phone and looking genuinely happy. As the sun set, James watched her laughing and splashing in the shallows as she spoke to Sophie, who was over 1000 kilometres away and yet right there with them. He was struck by the mystery of life. These remarkable women were without a doubt two of the most important people in his life, and yet only a couple of months ago he hadn't met either one of them. Tamara said goodbye to Sophie and started walking back over towards him.

'How was Sophie?' he asked.

'Wonderful. She is a wonderful person. It's not surprising that you're in love with her,' she said.

'I didn't say that I was in love with her.'

'You didn't have to. It's obvious.'

'Oh shit. How do I make her feel the same way?'

'What makes you think that she doesn't already feel the same way?'

'Because if she was in love with me, she would've said something by now. If someone is in love with someone else, they say something.'

'James, have you ever told her that you are in love with her?'

'Not yet. I don't want to scare her off. And what happens if I tell her that I'm in love with her and she feels completely differently?'

'She doesn't feel completely differently.'

'How do you know?'

'Because she told me she likes you. A lot. It seems one of the things you two have in common is your habit of telling everyone except each other how you feel.'

'Okay, I'm going to tell her. I'll tell her exactly how I feel the next time I see her. You are my witness. The next time I see Sophie, I'm telling her that I love her. Deal?'

'Deal.'

They lay back on the blanket drinking wine, listening to the waves and looking up at the stars as they talked about the future and the things the three of them would get up to at the Peggy Day Home.

'When will we go back?' asked James.

'I suppose we'll head back in a couple of days. We've done what we came to Byron to do.'

'Remind me – what exactly did we come here to do?'

'Have a holiday and drink wine on the grave of a dead friend, of course,' said Tamara. 'And I have a surprise for you tomorrow.'

'Can you tell me what it is?'

'Yes, I can,' she said. 'But I'm not going to.'

Eventually they picked up their stuff and wandered back to the hotel. In the foyer Phillip, the receptionist, asked James if he and his 'mother' would be having breakfast in the restaurant or up in their rooms the following morning.

'Put us down for eight-thirty in the restaurant,' interjected Tamara. 'We have a lot on tomorrow, and if my son is not up and eating by eight-thirty, he will sleep until midday. He's been like that ever since he was ten years old.'

'Mum,' complained James, 'I haven't slept like that for years.'

'Don't worry,' said Phillip. 'The family secrets are safe here with us!'

In the lift James and Tamara didn't say a word, but neither of them could stop smiling.

The next morning over breakfast Tamara seemed distracted.

'Are you okay?' asked James.

'Oh, my back has been giving me hell so I didn't sleep very well,' responded Tamara with a grimace.

'Should we go see a doctor?'

'No. A doctor would just tell me what they have all told me. I'm old and ill and I won't be getting any younger or better. Anyway, we haven't got time for doctors; today is your surprise.'

Just then Tamara's phone buzzed as she received a text. She read it and smiled.

'It's time.'

Just then came the unmistakable sound of a champagne cork being popped and a waiter appeared with a bottle of Dom Pérignon and some glasses.

'Tamara! This is so cool! Who doesn't like Dom? Especially in the morning. I don't know what I did to deserve this but . . . Thank you so much!'

'It's not from me,' said Tamara, still smiling.

'It's from the couple behind you,' said the waiter.

James turned around in his chair to thank whoever it was who had provided the champagne, and he shrieked. He shrieked for two reasons.

Reason #1: Usually when you are told someone is behind you they are at least a couple of metres away. These two people had snuck up and were about six inches behind James' head and grinning madly.

Reason #2: It was Cash Driveway and Sophie Glass.

A surprise indeed.

'Holy shit,' said James, getting up and hugging everyone in sight. 'Soph! Cash! This is the best! What are you doing here?'

'We were invited,' said a beaming Sophie, gesturing towards Tamara. 'Someone thought that you might like to see us.'

'I can't believe it. This is the best thing ever. How long are you staying?' asked James, still dancing around and hugging people. He even hugged the waiter who had just poured everyone champagne.

'We're here for a couple of days,' said Cash. 'You sounded like you were having way too much fun to not include us.' He looked around. 'This place is pretty cool. I think I could get used to it here.'

'You haven't seen anything yet, Mr Driveway,' said Tamara, shaking his hand by way of introduction. 'Come and look at the view. I hope you brought some paint and brushes.' With that Tamara led Cash through the dining room and out onto one of the balconies. 'I hope you two don't mind if we leave you alone for a minute?' she said over her shoulder to the still beaming Sophie and James.

'We'll be fine,' said Sophie.

'Yes,' added James, 'no rush.'

The two of them stood there, taking each other in.

'God, I've missed you,' said James. 'I had no idea that you were coming.'

'I know. I've missed you too, and in the last couple of days, whenever we spoke, it took every bit of my self-control not to blurt out, "We're coming to meet you! I'll see you in two days!" If Tamara wasn't in her seventies, I'd be quite jealous. In fact, I'm quite jealous anyway. And I'm so proud of you. You should hear the way she talks about you on the phone. You've made this trip everything that it could be for her. She adores you.'

'I adore her! She's the best. Well, I mean, *you're* the best, but she's pretty fucking cool. And she's always telling me what I should and shouldn't do when it comes to you.'

'Like what?'

'Well, like the other day I told her that I loved you.' James downed half a glass of champagne in one awkward swallow.

'What did she say to that?' asked Sophie, unintentionally moving from one foot to the other. She kind of knew that he loved her, but he'd never said it before. Now he had. It was one of those things that can't be unsaid. She took the remaining half-glass of champagne from James and finished it.

'She said that I should tell you as soon as I saw you next.'

'Do you think you will tell me?'

'I doubt it. I'm too shy.'

'Fair enough. And if you did tell me, I'd probably just say some-thing like, "And I love you too, you massive idiot." And that's just predictable.'

James' face lit up. *Did she just say that? She just said that.* He was smiling so much it almost hurt. He took the empty glass from her hand and put it down on the table. 'I'll fill this up in a minute,' he said as they came together in a hug that was so meant to be that they virtually disappeared into each other.

'But now we've both said it. I love you, Sophie Glass.'

'You know James, if this was a film, this would be the bit where we kissed.'

'I agree. It totally would be. I reckon even if it was just a book this is the bit where we would kiss.'

'Probably . . . Books are like that.'

They kissed.

After a few seconds the kiss was interrupted by a voice asking, 'More champagne?'

It was the waiter.

'Um . . . Sure,' said Sophie, feeling equal parts happy and exposed.

'Sir?' the waiter asked James.

'That would be great,' he said, before adding, 'You know, we were just kissing.'

'I know,' said the waiter, looking embarrassed. 'It's just, you were chatting and I came to fill your glasses, but just as I was going to ask, you said something about books and then started kissing and I was kind of stuck standing there with the bottle. So I thought, "Let them have the best bit of the kiss, and *then* ask . . ."'

'And the first bit of a kiss is the best bit,' said Sophie.

'Yes. At least usually,' said the waiter. 'I mean, some people probably love the end bit of kissing, but I prefer the beginning. It's all about potential. I do feel like a bit of a killjoy now, though.'

'Oh, no. Don't feel like that. You definitely let us have the best bit. Don't you agree, Soph?'

'Yes. For sure. It was a great kiss but, to be honest, it had peaked.'

'Would you like a glass yourself?' Sophie asked the waiter. He looked around carefully to see if anyone was watching.

'I'd love one.'

Sophie picked up a glass from the table and the waiter filled it. They all clinked a toast and had a much-needed drink.

That night, Tamara, Cash, Sophie and James met in the foyer bar for a martini before heading out to a dinner that Tamara had organised for them. On the beach, a table had been set up for the four of them. It was beautiful. Flowers had been arranged and smelled like heaven. Candles burned. The only thing that could have made it even better was if Malcolm was sitting under a palm tree playing the cello. They reached the table as a waiter poured them all champagne and waves rolled calmly shoreward.

As the others sat down, Tamara stood strongly (no doubt aided to some degree by painkillers) and embarked on a speech, framed by the glory of a Byron Bay sunset.

'I am going to speak. I am going to speak about you. I've paid for dinner, so the least you can do is humour me by listening. To begin with, I am thrilled that we are all here, especially Sophie and Cash. Please don't misunderstand me; seeing James has become a daily thrill but to have all three of you here together has its own special joy.'

James was about to comment on Tamara's sarcasm when he realised that she was being completely straight. As I have mentioned earlier there was a certain nobility to Tamara Higginson, and that nobility was enhanced when she was being sincere. This was one of those times.

'The lives of others, you see, have rarely dragged me in. But after driving all this way, listening to James talking of the two of you, I have become compelled. I am left feeling that the whole point of life is other people. Is closeness. Is friendship.

'Sophie, if you feel anything for James that approaches what he feels for you, then you have a friend (clearly more than a friend) for life. There is something quite beautiful about hearing a smart-arse like James melt as he talks, or even thinks, about someone else. And in this case that someone else is you. You are a couple, you just haven't had time to acknowledge it yet.

'Cash and James, you are so very lucky to have each other in your lives. Whenever I have heard one of you speak of the other, what I hear more than anything else is unmitigated joy. You see each other's lunacy and madness, but you also see each other's potential and wonder. You would truly do anything for each other, and that is what I consider to be true love.'

James was surprised that he didn't have anything smart-arsed to say about the 'true love' that he and Cash apparently shared. Perhaps Tamara's sincerity was rubbing off on him.

Cash was moved by Tamara's declaration as well. He was almost twice James' age and felt at once both older and younger than his friend. Cash often thought of love as the shared experience of feelings that didn't need explanation. If this was in fact what love was, then Cash loved James without reservation.

As they continued drinking and eating the night became something of a thank-you frenzy. Tamara thanked James for joining her on their adventure, and for being so understanding about not actually getting to meet Baylor Petersen. Sophie and Cash thanked Tamara for the unexpected trip. James (a little drunkenly) thanked everyone for everything, but mostly thanked Tamara for something that he couldn't quite define. Something life-changing. She had taught him much about friendship and he intended to spend as much time with his new friend as he possibly could. Before the inevitable. Before the end. But that was a long way into the future, and the present was plenty.

That night Sophie and James did it.

They made love, had sex, fucked, got it on, or what have you. And according to both of them, it was wonderful.

I could go into detail but as I wasn't there and as neither of them would appreciate me telling you what they told me in confidence, let's just be happy to know that they did eventually get to the place that they had both been wanting to get to from very early on.

We can all let out a relieved sigh.

I'm sure they both did.

Hooray for love. Hooray for sex.

Hooray for Sophie and James.

The next morning Sophie and James got up together, dressed and headed down for breakfast. James was bouncing and dancing around like a puppy. You could safely say that he was pleased to have woken up in the same bed as Sophie.

'Do you have the feeling that everyone we pass knows what we did last night?' he asked.

'No,' said Sophie. 'But it's pretty wild to know that your self-obsession runs so deep that you think people would even care.'

'Are we going to have our first fight?' he asked as they got into the lift and Sophie kissed him into silence.

'No,' she said. 'We had that ages ago.'

As they wandered into the breakfast area they saw Cash at a small table surrounded by about twenty staff members and guests.

'I don't know what Cash is doing or has done, but try to find Tamara,' said James nervously. 'We may have to leave here fairly quickly.'

'Oh, I don't know,' said Sophie as they approached the scene. 'No one looks angry. Nothing is on fire. Everything might be fine.'

And fine it was.

They could hear the observers 'oohing' and 'ahhing' appreciatively as they got closer to Cash's table. They arrived just in time to see him putting the finishing touches on what was a remarkable reproduction of the view from the balcony, from one end of the beach right around to the lighthouse. Cash had made his interpretation of this scene using nothing but the rinds and husks of the various fruits that were available in the buffet. The fruits were the paint and the tablecloth was the canvas. Waves were formed from the rinds of honeydew melons. Brown sugar was sand. There were even surfboats carved from apple with the surf lifesavers wearing little orange lifejackets made from little orange oranges. The whole thing was so perfectly Cash Driveway. A work of genius that could not possibly last more than an hour or two. People were taking photos of the art and the artist. Children were bringing him the last few pieces of fruit that he needed to finish the work. Cash would tell them the size and shape of what he needed and the children would gleefully chew away in an attempt to provide him with exactly what he required. One set of happy parents commented that their child had probably eaten more fruit that morning than he had in his entire life. Any fear of James' that the management would be angry at the mess Cash was making was quickly forgotten when both the manager and the chef insisted on getting a photograph with Cash and his creation.

'Cash! That is beautiful!' said Sophie.

'Thanks, Sophie. Have you got any idea how much fruit I had to eat to even get this started? If it wasn't for my fellow diners we would never have got anywhere near completing this.'

'Well, you certainly won't be getting scurvy any time soon,' said James, smiling at the beauty of his friend's creation.

'Hey, James, look who's in the bottom corner.'

And there she was. Made from white bread and brown crust. A little creature that simply had to be Charlie Girl. She even had a tiny green ball in her mouth made out of apple skin.

'Where's Tamara? She has to see this,' said Cash.

'She hasn't been down yet?'

'Not that I've seen,' said Cash. 'Mind you, I've been – doing this.' He swept an arm in the direction of his artwork.

'Maybe she's sleeping in. It was a big night,' said Sophie.

'Not for her,' replied James. 'There is no night big enough to slow that woman down.'

'Maybe you should check on her,' said Cash.

'Yeah, okay. Back in a minute. Don't let anyone chuck that out; she'll want to see it,' said James as he headed back to the elevator.

When he got to Tamara's room he saw a note on her door, and he also noticed that the door was being held open with a towel. The note, handwritten and stuck to the 'Do Not Disturb' sign, read: 'James. It looks like I'll be flying home after all. Thank you for everything.'

He knew before he pushed the door open.

Tamara Higginson was gone.

*

The room smelled of incense she had bought in town and Patti Smith was playing on the stereo. The bedside light was on and she lay on her back with the hint of a smile on her face. There was another note addressed to James on the bedside table, next to a half-empty bottle of vodka and the blue container that she kept her painkillers in. James picked it up and shook it. It was empty. Yesterday, when James had seen it at breakfast, it had been full.

For the first time in his life James found himself hoping that there was something after death, and in Tamara's case he hoped that thing was Baylor Petersen. His eyes started to tear up but then he stopped. There would be time for crying. There would be time for lots of stuff. There seemed no rush to do anything. For a moment he felt the urge to talk, to tell her everything, everything important, and then he smiled as he realised he already had.

At some point he called Sophie. A minute or two later she and Cash were with James in the room, Sophie holding James and Cash sitting on the bed holding Tamara's hand. They stayed with her as long as they needed to and then they called the hotel manager, who in turn called the authorities.

'We are all so sorry, sir. Your mother was such a wonderful person,' said the manager to James.

'Yes,' said James. 'Yes, she was.'

After everyone had left, James, Sophie and Cash went downstairs and drank martinis. They figured that is what Tamara would have wanted. They were right.

'Do you think she ever intended to leave here?' asked Cash. 'Was she ever going to move out of her place and into the home?'

'No,' said Sophie. 'She wanted to see Baylor. Maybe she was telling him that she was on her way to join him.'

'She left me this,' said James, producing the letter he'd found on the bedside table.

'Please read it slowly,' said Cash.

'Why slowly?' asked Sophie.

'Because this is it. I know we haven't known her for long, but this is the last time we'll hear from her . . . I know it sounds dumb but I want her to last.'

'You're right. I won't rush her.'

And with that James read the first and last letter he would ever get from Tamara Higginson.

Dearest James,

I don't know if you expected me to do this, but I hope not; after all, no one wants to be predictable. I assume you know that this was not an act of sorrow or desperation. It was simply a stubborn old lady going out, her own way, in her own time. I had been planning this for months before I met you. I was way more ill than any of you, or anyone beside my doctor, knew. I only had a couple of months left, even if I'd let this happen organically. This wasn't an act of sorrow; it was release. Letting go. The only place I was ever going to go was to snuggle down next to Baylor Petersen in the little racist cemetery on the hill.

I have left various letters with my attorney in Melbourne making it clear that I will be buried here, next to Baylor, regardless of what Catherine wants. It's my body; it will go where I want it to. And I want the three of you to handle the arrangements for my funeral.

I have also taken a few liberties with Sophie, Cash and yourself. You'll have to go to see my lawyer; I've included his details.

First, I want you to take the car. You are virtually the only person who has driven it in the last few years and you obviously enjoyed it, so that is done. It is yours. Shut up.

Second, I left a sum of money for Sophie to spend on the Peggy Day Home in whichever way she sees fit. She actually cares for other people, and that is to be celebrated. You will never meet a more caring person. For god's sake, she even cares for you and Cash. That speaks volumes.

I have told my lawyer to give Cash as much money as he needs to build a 'big' thing. Something along the lines of the Big Orange, the Big Pineapple or the Big Koala. I want it to be something that pleases half the people who see it and infuriates the rest . . .

'Consider it done,' said Cash.

My final act is this – and while it's aimed at you, James, nothing would make me happier than to have all three of you involved with it.

Last week I had someone make an offer for the Majestic cinema, and the offer was accepted. The cinema now belongs to James Rogers and there is money set aside to renovate and maintain it.

A week ago you came into my home pretending to be my son and, though it sounds bizarre, in the last several years, few things have made me as happy. If I have brought even half as much joy to your life as you brought to mine, I die a very happy woman. Which reminds me, I better stop writing as I took the pills half an hour ago and I just remembered that I'm dying. Just so that you know, dying doesn't feel bad. It actually feels like . . .

There was a long pause.

'What?' said Cash. 'Dying feels like what?'

'I don't know. That's all she wrote.'

'What? She can't leave it there! I reckon she's just deliberately holding out on us.'

'I'm going to have to agree with Cash on this one. I sense a certain degree of joy in her not letting on,' said Sophie.

It was only after he had finished reading that James realised he was crying. They all were. Three people standing in a hotel bar bawling their eyes out. Something had to change. Sophie raised her martini.

'To Tamara,' she said.

'To Tamara,' repeated James. 'The greatest pretend mother I ever had.'

Five days later Tamara Higginson was buried next to Baylor Petersen in the least racist part of the beautiful Bangalow Cemetery. It was a wonderful service. There were about thirty people there, and, importantly, Catherine came. When James first laid eyes on her he felt an odd combination of anger and fear, but he needn't have. She simply walked up to him with tears in her eyes, put her arms around him, and said, 'You made her happier than you will never know. Thank you.'

A couple of days after the funeral it was decided that the three of them would drive back to Melbourne using the same car and the same route that James and Tamara had used to get to Byron.

On their way out of town, they stopped in Bangalow and bought a two-litre cask of reasonably brutal white wine and some plastic glasses. After pouring a little wine onto the graves of Baylor and Tamara, they sat down and drank and talked.

'Have you decided what "big" thing you're going to make?' Sophie asked Cash.

'I'm not sure yet,' he replied. 'I'm thinking maybe a 200-foot-tall bowl of tom yum soup out of various coloured clothes pegs, and, if I can get permission, I'd install it on the roof of Graham's restaurant.'

'Yeah,' said James. 'I like it: "The Thai-tanic, Home of the Big Tom Yum".'

Just then Cash's phone buzzed. He read something on the screen and then watched a short video that had accompanied the message.

'Holy shit,' he said as he watched. 'Holy, holy shit.'

'What is it?' asked Sophie.

'I think you are going to like this,' he said to her. 'Remember the email that I sent you, the one about Mrs Murphy standing out by her tree?'

'Yes,' said Sophie.

'Remember I said I had a friend who was a private investigator, Ken Rosalind?'

'Yes, Cash, I remember.'

'Well, Ken went looking for her children, for the twins. I assumed he would never find them . . .'

'What are you saying, Cash?'

Cash handed his phone to Sophie and she and James watched what Ken had sent. It was a video shot on the grounds of the Peggy Day Home. It showed Mrs Murphy standing as she did every morning by her tree, and it looked no different from any other day. But then something happened. Something that hadn't happened before. Two people appeared in the corner of the frame. A man and a woman, both in their forties. And slowly, gently, they approached Mrs Murphy.

'Oh god,' whispered Sophie. 'Please let this be real.'

There was a cautious moment as the two people stood in front of Mrs Murphy, not knowing what to do, before slowly she reached out to them and they fell into her arms.

Like a mother and her children.

Like a family.

Sophie, James and Cash took their time on the drive back to Melbourne. What was there to hurry for? James felt a certain responsibility introducing the other two to the mysteries of life on the Tamara highway. And he took that responsibility very seriously. He shared the story of their journey to Byron with Cash and Sophie as they fed toast to a horse over a wire fence by the side of the road. And, though James was telling the story, the other two were hearing every word of it in the strong, bright, beautiful voice of Tamara Higginson.

And how do I know all of this happened?

How do I know that any of it occurred?

I know it because my name is Cash Driveway, and, as your humble narrator, I was there, people.

I was there.

ACKNOWLEDGEMENTS

This book would not have happened without the remarkable support of the following people:

Roz Hammond for the inspiration, the love and the belief. I'm sorry.

Pauline Davies for encouraging me when I first thought of the story, and for being the kind of parent that I wish I had been.

David Rogers for the roof and the roasts.

Kristen Fleet for taking care of our mother to the end.

Tony Martin for refusing to be pressured into turning on his friends for the simple crime of falling in love.

Sophy Blake for friendship, vodka and art.

My wonderful editor Cate Blake for cutting out the waffle.

Josh Durham for designing a cover that so perfectly captures the story.

Malcolm Hill for coming up with the greatest name ever: Cash Driveway.

Frehd Southern-Starr, stay gold.

Charlie Girl, the best dog ever.

All the authors, filmmakers and musicians who continue to inspire me.

And finally to Ian Darling, for the kindness, wisdom and generosity. A great man, a great artist and a great friend.